A ThorStruck Publication

Published by ThorStruck Press in 2012

Copyright © 2011 Poppet

All rights reserved. No part of this book may be reproduced, stored in a retrieval system or transmitted in any form or by any means without the prior written permission of the publishers, except by a reviewer who may quote brief passages in a review to be printed by a newspaper, magazine or journal.

First Print Edition

All characters appearing in this work are fictitious. Any resemblance to real persons, living or dead, is purely coincidental.

ISBN-13: 978-1479173976

ISBN-10: 1479173975

Djinn

by
Poppet

Djinn

 **Prologue**

It's really dark. Can't see anything. Not even my hand.
It's warm too, and stuffy. Reaching a hand out, I feel the confining walls. They're like wallpaper.
Where am I?
"Hello!"
"Can anyone hear me?!"
Nothing.
It doesn't feel like a coffin. What does a coffin feel like?
I don't remember anything.
How the hell did I get here?
It's too small. I can't move around.
Oh God, I think I've been buried alive.
Wait.
Can you hear that?
Sounds like voices.
"Hello!"
Getting louder now. I can see a faint light.
"Help! Somebody please help me!"
The lid lifts.

Poppet

Djinn

 Chapter 1

Cindy:

My gaze follows the letters as the planchette grazes the surface in a soothing rattle. I can't start my day without answers.

Today's question is: Tell me what I need to be happy?

The words spell, S-A-S-H-A.

"A book at Sasha's?"

I half expect it to say Bible.

The planchette jiggles in spurts, wood tapping on wood, dancing so fast across the board it's now taking my full concentration.

P-A-R-A-D-I-C-E

I never have to knock on wood starting each day with such an auspicious ritual.

"Thanks. Good-bye."

The pointer skims across to Good-bye, ending our morning session. Glancing at the time, I have just enough of a gap for another cup of coffee before heading to work.

The only upside to my job, is my love for books. Here I am surrounded with thousands of the things, but all I can think about is, what is so special waiting for me at Para-Dice?

What will my favorite occult bookstore have in stock, that I

Poppet

can't find right here? I'm far too impatient to wait until after work to visit my favorite haunt; what if I wait and someone else gets *the* book of my dreams, I can't risk it. Waiting the last ten minutes to lunch hour is torturous, tapping my pen against the keyboard, I glare at the tiny block showing the time.

Oh look, email.

Clicking on it, I wait for it to open.

Hey Cinders, are you coming to church tonight?
Reply:
Yup, I'll be there. I'm going early though. Why? Do you need a lift?

Send.

I glance impatiently at the time again, then up at the library. I have a perfect view from my office of rows of shelves, stacked high with the best aromatherapy on earth. Nothing beats opening a book and inhaling. New print or old print, it's a heady experience.

When you open a new book it's personal, like an exchange of secrets, almost like holding someone's hand for the first time. For me, it's an intense religious experience, brimming with hope, and a rendezvous between just the two of you, which is private and personal.

It's normally quiet on a Monday morning, but lunch hour is about to happen and I don't plan on being caught at my workstation and working half my lunch-hour away for these saps.

I may do admin, but every time someone closes an account, opens one, or a new shipment comes in, I have to work. Judy has a job to do too, it's time she bloody did some work around here.

Shuffling my oracle cards one last time before heading out, I close my eyes and concentrate.

Great Spirit, show me the way.

Flicking over the top three cards, I stare at Salamander, Lunessa and Mysteria. Thumbing through the pages of the

Djinn

divination explanations to Salamander, I read:

Fire is all around you now. You have the blessing of the fire spirit, Salamander, to guide your way.

Lunessa: Mother Moon is unseen in day. Use her light to guide your way. Auspicious for new beginnings, rituals and blessings.

Mysteria: You have stumbled onto great mystery. You are chosen to work and weave the mysterious. The unseen behind the seen protect you. Accept the unexpected. With great insight comes greater responsibility and power.

Well it's about time. Protection **and** power. Way overdue.

I snap the Oracle closed and shove the cards and the book into my voluminous bag. Standing and pushing my chair back under my desk, I lean over it to lock the computer with my password, and catapult for the door.

"See you in an hour," I say, as I past the matronly slacker with the thick spectacles.

By the time Judy puts her finger in the book she's reading and looks up, I'm already skipping down the steps to the paid parking lot, down the road from Portland's Central Library.

Normally I'd take the number fourteen bus to work, but because I was planning on going to church after work, I brought the car today. And depending on what's in store for me, I might just end up going to church at a normal time after all.

It doesn't take me long because all I have to do is drive north down 10th Avenue, turn into Alder, then take the Morrison bridge over the river to Belmont, and go round the block from 55th Avenue. The store is just before the corner of Southeast Hawthorne Boulevard and Market.

Parking in a back road, I look across at the converted old house with a mystical signboard over the gable announcing Para-

Poppet

Dice. Walking under the two dice with the number six showing on both of their transparent ruby cubes, I inhale the familiar scent of sandalwood incense.

Stepping through the red fringe hanging down from the threshold, I wait for my eyes to adjust.

"Mon cheri, how are you?"

He always gives me a smile. I'm positive he's a stoner who spends most of his days locating the next high, but he has a knack for finding rare and unusual books.

Walking over to him, I absently fluff my white hair with new pink streaks. I wonder if he'll notice.

"Hi Sasha, you're looking surprisingly sober for a Monday." Fingering the blue tiger's-eye on a leather strap around my neck, I lean a hip against the counter and stare into his gray eyes.

"And you're looking very pink."

He noticed.

"Do you like it?" I ask.

"I like you best when you're just shocking blond. I like you shocking. Pink is too sweet for you."

"Are you saying I'm not sweet?"

"You are my precious arsenic, cheri. I like you bitter, and one day," he pauses with a smirk wringing his lips, "I shall witness you twisted."

"You're such a charmer."

"Give in, I never give up," he winks.

"Something tells me you're hiding a new book which you've saved just for me."

"How do you always know my surprises? Hmm? Where did you hide the camera? Because of you I'm too afraid to masturbate in here."

"Good god, I should bloody hope not. How to ruin fabulous novels."

"I'm teasing," he grins, while a hand snakes under the table section of the counter.

"If you've got it out and were whacking off, I'll leave and never come back."

"Cindy! You shock even me."

His hand withdraws and he stands along with the motion, proving his jeans are zipped up. In his left hand is a very thick and aged book. No longer distracted by his purple and blue tie-dyed t-shirt and hidden hand, I am drawn to the vellum covered manuscript. Inhaling deeply, a warmth flutters through me with butterflies and exhilaration.

"What is it?"

"Agree to Saturday night, and it's yours."

"How much?"

He shakes his head. His stare unwavering. "Agree, or no dice baby."

"Let me touch it first," I insist.

His free hand flirts briefly with the zipper on his jeans, before he bursts out laughing, "I've longed to hear those words from such vibrantly neon-pink lips."

"Shut the fuck up."

Despite him joking, it's taking all my resolve to not blush. He places the book between us on the mahogany counter, scuffed with age and probably jewelry. Resting my left hand next to his on the four inch thick book, I feel it, breathing slowly, testing the vibrations. Heat chases up my arm, swirls around my heart, before unsettling me with a sensation of lust which I haven't experienced in ages.

Narrowing my eyes, I watch Sasha, deciding if he's using the book as a channel, or if this is really only the book. He misreads the concentrated glare and lifts his hand as if I'm pointing a gun at him. Jubilation jolts me, I've never had such desperation, I have to have it.

Nodding, gripping the semi-precious stone around my neck

tighter, "Okay. I'll go out with you."

He hands it over, it's heavy. Closing my eyes, I pries it open just enough to smell the pages, there's a spicy redolence wafting from it. Opening my eyes as I shut it again, I stare at the bold gold lettering on the cover of the mustard hued binding, 'Djinn'; it's glorious.

"Okay, why this one?" I ask, touching the binding with a lover's caress.

"I know you and oracle books, this one is in a league of its own."

Snapping my focus back to Sasha's stubbled face, I scrutinize his expression. It didn't sound like he was judging me, but it doesn't hurt to check.

"Relax sweetheart, when I get you twisted, I'll show you a different kind of divination."

"Yeah, penis dowsing no doubt."

His laughter cracks the tension, it's warm and indulgent, seduction all its own.

"How come we've never gone out for coffee?" I ask him.

"Because you're a stuck up bitch who likes losers."

I laugh back at his teasing.

"Losers you say? But then, you qualify," I grin at him.

"Ha, thanks. And we're not doing coffee, I'm getting you wasted on body shots – that's a guarantee," he adds.

Arching a dark eyebrow at him; that's a challenge if I've ever heard one. "We'll see. Now, how much do I owe you?"

"For Djinn? On the house, I'll get my pay on Saturday."

"Shees you're a cocky bastard."

"Cocked and aimed."

Rolling my eyes, I offer him a sweet syrupy smile, "Aw, do you charm all the girls the way you lay it on me?"

His expression loses its congeniality, "You are the only woman I'd waste this much time on."

Djinn

"Why?"

He points at the book, "Because you understand."

"Meaning?"

"You have a knack for the esoteric. Without being flakey or trendy about it."

Leaning both elbows on the counter, I watch him flick his overgrown sandy hair out of his eyes, "Have you ever considered going to the church, La Comtesse de la Nuit?"

"Haha, I knew you were a twisted woman. If I wanted to sell my soul, I'd sell it to you, not that crowd of fakers."

Insulted, I withdraw, "Thanks for the book, I have to go."

"Cindy," he calls after me when I reach the fringed curtain.

I turn back to stare at him, "What?"

"I'll pick you up at nine."

"Okay."

He gives me a nuclear powerful smile and instinctively I smile back. With my new book, I head back out into dazzling sunlight and my Mini, which desperately needs a wash.

Sitting behind the steering wheel, I unearth the quartz pendulum from my bag. Holding it, dangling from the silver chain between me and the dash, I wait for it to steady.

"Should I go out with Sasha on Saturday night? Circle right for yes, left for no." It begins to make incremental movements before violently swinging in a clockwise ring; then abruptly stops.

Palming it, I say, "Thanks." Putting it back into the pink silk bag I keep it in for vibrational purity, I tuck it safely in my purse and pull on the safety belt. Slipping on my sunglasses and starting the engine, I glance back at the faded blue house and spy Sasha watching me from the upstairs window.

I lift my hand to indicate farewell before engaging first gear and pulling off, Djinn snugly weighing down my lap like a kitten about to claw.

⛧

 Chapter 2

Cindy:

The moment I get home, I sit down in the lounge, kick off my shoes, and open Djinn.

Frowning, I stare at the first page after turning the initial few empty, aged yellow, pages.

Are you Ready?

What is that supposed to mean? What a dumb way to start a book.

I thumb to the next page.

I asked, are you Ready?

Paging back, I double check the first page.

This is an interactive book, changing pages won't help you answer the question.

Holy crap.

As I'm staring, the words fade and are replaced again with the first question. I feel utterly stupid speaking to a book. "Ready for what?"

For your life to change.

"I'm ready for my life to change, for the better."

Then turn the page.

Oh come on, this has to be a joke. Sasha's messing with me.

Yet I am apprehensive as I flip the page.

I am Djinn. I'm here to bring to fruition your deepest

Djinn

cravings. I will manifest your greatest desires and give you the power you've been seeking.

"What have I been seeking?"

Smart-ass book.

You have been searching for happiness. For meaning, direction and power.

"What's in it for you?"

There's always a catch.

Freedom.

"From what?"

This book.

"What are you?"

For lack of a better term, a genie.

"But I thought genies only grant three wishes."

Don't believe everything you read. I am powerful and can conjure anything you wish; and change your bad luck, finally.

For every answer I thumb to the next page. It's nuts, but I doubt I'll read the same book twice no matter how many times I read Djinn.

Looking around, I'm still thinking this is a con. They've put hidden cameras in my home, waiting to see me make a complete fool of myself.

Time to test it.

"Boil the kettle, I want coffee."

The kettle behind me in the open plan kitchen pops on and starts to make all the right heating noises.

Dropping the book on the vacant spot next to me, I back away and stare at it. This is beyond bizarre and now I'm getting the jeeblies.

It bounces onto the floor, open in the middle.

Inching closer, I stare at bold black words, flicking my attention around again, waiting for someone to yell 'gotcha'.

Power at your fingertips, yet when you finally have it in

Poppet

your grasp you lack conviction. Take me back to Paradise.
"It's not Paradise, it's Para-dice."
No. It is Paradise. Open your eyes, or are you always this blind?
"Screw you."
Pages whirr in frenetic turning before stopping. Gold motes cloud the book as if someone just bashed it with a powder puff loaded with edible glitter.
You are not worthy, Sasha is.
You have failed.
The binding creaks as the book slams shut.
"Jesus."
Beyond freaked out, I leap off my chair backwards over the armrest. Dashing for my bedroom, I rush in and huddle on the bed, hugging my knees, thinking.
I still have to go to church, but Djinn has made me feel tainted.
That was a mind fuck if ever I've witnessed one.
Annoyed, using rage as a shield, I stomp to the bathroom and begin drawing my bath. Selecting the Spiritually Divine bath oil, I measure out a portion of the purple liquid infused with sandalwood, myrrh, frankincense and cinnamon.
Whisking to the left, I pick up the Zippo and light the white Purification candle imbedded with lumps of dragon's blood. Almost satisfied, I flounce back to the bedroom and retrieve the portable CD player. Closing the door on Djinn, disrobing, I press play and blast Inkubus Sukkubus into the pale peach room.
Paranoid, I drape my shirt over the bathroom mirror, just to be on the safe side. I have exactly twenty minutes to bathe and get dressed. I'll just have to deal with that freaky book after church.

It's just gone seven when I enter the Sacred Church of La Comtesse de la Nuit. Jaques waits just inside the door, the lighting

Djinn

dim and barely catching the highlights of the thick blue velvet curtains on each window in the converted house, the censor is waved around my head before he sprinkles ash on my hair.

Leaning forward he kisses me on each cheek, "May the Great Spirit bless you tonight."

"Thanks Jaques."

Fluffing the holy ash out of my hair, I make my way to the right, to the empty chair next to Rachel. Blowing up at my eyelashes to dislodge more ash, I slip into the vacant spot.

"Hey," I whisper to her.

She leans her head toward mine, "Where have you been?"

"Purification ritual, got spooked."

She gives me an odd look before murmuring, "You smell good, what is it?"

"Patchouli oil."

"From Para-Dice?"

I nod, hushing as La Comtesse de la Nuit enters the platform from the left of the room where a black door sways ajar.

She holds up a hand, drawing her tapestry shawl in peacock colors around her tighter, "Silence."

I lean to the left to get a better look at her, because the man with the camel posture in front of me has such curly wild hair, I can't see anything. The lights turn out from the back and only the candles on either side of the front of the room illuminate her now. I recall reading in an interview ages ago run in the local paper, that her real name is Ingrid; I don't blame her for changing it.

She gestures wildly to the left of us, "Over here, close to the back, one of you. I have a message from an elderly woman, smells like lavender, recently passed over ..." She rubs her chest above gigantic matronly boobs, "Had a bad chest. I don't think it was breast cancer, more like an infection, or emphysema. Possibly lung cancer."

A middle aged woman with chestnut hair styled in a bob

bursts into tears, saying loudly to her companions, "It's Sally."

The Comtesse throws her head back theatrically, lifting both hands; trembling. Her shawl slides to the floor and she stands with her squat body draped in a long black dress centre stage.

"Yes, that's it. She has a message for you ..."

Her eyes pop open, bulbous and wide as she points a viciously painted taloned finger at the sobbing woman who is currently shoving her nose in a hanky, "You are surrounded with angels. There is light all around you. She says; do not worry, you are divinely protected, and the issues worrying you will be resolved with love."

"Thank you, thank you," mumbles the stupid waffling loser.

The Comtesse's hand catches my eye with the huge amber ring on it as she lifts her other hand and marches to our side.

"Someone over here. Name beginning with a T. A man ..."

Camel posture lifts his hand. Fuck, now I definitely can't see anything.

"A little girl, name beginning with an M. Mary, or ..."

"Yes, it's Mary. How is she? What does she say?"

Leaning to the left, I look around him to the leader of the spiritualist church as she says, "And you are? Tom? Am I right?"

"Yes ..."

Oh god, why does everyone come here just to cry? They're dead, get over it.

"She says she loves you very much and misses you terribly, but you mustn't worry because she's safe and happy with Delores."

He bows his head, wracking, shoulders shaking so much that I'm just getting pissed off. I can't see anything because of his hulk heaving about, and I am totally grossed out with the snot noises coming from him.

"Can we move?" I whisper to Rachel.

She nods, and we get up and shuffle over to the left side of

Djinn

the room.

"You! Girl with the white hair!"

Frozen, I straighten my spine and face her, pointing at myself.

"Yes you! Jean, Jeanie, something like that, has a message for you."

Rachel's ogling me and sinks into the empty vinyl chair beside mine. I determinedly say nothing, facing the woman at the front waggling her finger about in my direction.

"It's now or never. It's time for you to choose. You won't get another opportunity like this one."

I continue to face her, remaining obstinately silent.

See people, no crying. If I can do it, you can do it.

She pales severely, making the rouge on her cheeks highlight like clown's make-up, "Or you will burn. **Burn!**"

She collapses and the lights turn up, barely enough to navigate with. Jacques scurries to the front, pawing at the air as he reaches her, "Someone help me move her to her chambers."

I give Rachel a shrug in answer to her questioning eyebrows.

Staring at the dark paintings between the curtains showing Jesus and Mary independently, with bright yellow circles behind their heads, I'm distracted again when someone shouts, "We must sing a hymn of praise."

"Should we duck?" I ask Rachel.

I'm finding this annoying tonight.

She nods, grabbing our bags together in one hand and following my rush up the centre aisle to the door at the rear next to books and CD's on mediumship.

Bursting through into the clean air outside, I violently scuff my hair to dislodge the ash left in it.

"I need a smoke."

Rachel already has her box out and lights one for me too, handing it to over, "Who the hell is Jeany?"

Inhaling deeply from the cigarette, I tilt my head back against the trunk of the tree where we're halted, staring up, "A book."

"A book gave you a message from beyond the grave?"

"Yup." Exhaling, I look at Raych, all gypsy looking, right down to the hoops in her ears. "Fancy going out for a drink?"

"I can't. Derrick is coming over tonight. He had a fight with his mom again and is making noises about moving in."

I nod again. I don't really feel like being alone.

"Well tonight was short and sweet, you must be thrilled," I say instead. The lucky bitch is getting laid tonight.

Mesmerising brown eyes that look halfway between Mexican and Mediterranean blink at me, "You okay?"

"Peachy." I offer an empty smile, "Go. I'll be fine."

She leans in and hugs me, "I love you, take care."

Inclining my head, I keep the supportive smile stuck to my face until she is out of sight.

Drawing deeply from the cigarette, I unearth my cell phone and skim through the numbers. Finding Sasha's, as he lives in the same house as the bookstore, I press dial and begin walking to the Mini.

"'Sup?"

"It's Cindy you big dork."

"Cinders! To what do I owe such a divine pleasure?"

"I don't feel like being alone and Djinn scared the crap out of me."

"My bed is big enough for three, who're ya bringin'?"

"Myself. Your place or mine?"

"Yours."

"Ha!" I flick the butt into the centre of the road and stare at the full moon, "I just need a friend tonight, Sash."

"Do you have rocket fuel?"

"Some, doesn't hurt to bring more."

"Catch you in twenty, babe."

"See you then."

Djinn

I disconnect and open the car, getting in, clenching my jaw, determined I'm being stupid and freaking out over nothing.

With my hands gripping the steering wheel, I ignore the tension in my diaphragm, choosing instead to blare NIN into the cosy confines while I initiate the engine for lift off - and wonder why the swollen moon makes me think something big is going to happen tonight.

Chapter 3

Cindy:

I know Sasha has my address because it's on record at Para-Dice. I live in an apartment on SE 37th Ave on the corner of Market street, literally a few blocks away from him in Hawthorne.

It's with relief that I spy his tall lanky frame propped up by a shoulder outside my front door.

I give him a smile as I slip the key in the lock, "You don't waste any time."

"Time is of the essence."

Pushing the white door open, I switch on the lights and wait for him to enter before closing and locking it. He looks around at the Bohemian décor in reds, scarlet, navy and gold, scrutinizing my face.

"I didn't figure you as having opulent taste."

"It reminds me of the colors used in ancient manuscripts. Like the illumination done by medieval monks. That's why."

He moves to the kitchen, depositing Apia, a honey vodka by Artisan Spirits, and Absinthe made by Gnostalgic Spirits, plus Vanillia Espresso Vodka by Elemental, onto the kitchen counter. It's organic and made in Portland.

How did he end up choosing my favorites? That's just too weird.

Gobsmacked, I watch him pile more bottles out onto the

Djinn

counter. All locally made, but now he's hit the sweet spot with Lovejoy. Absently licking my lips, I stare at the full bottle of hazelnut vodka, which he follows with sugar cubes for the absinthe. He even has another bottle of absinthe by Trillium. True anarchist drinking is on the table tonight. He wasn't kidding, I guess he plans to add me to 'on the table tonight' too.

Or flat out on the floor.

He makes himself at home, stalking long legs to the kitchen cupboards, opening them one by one to locate glasses.

Turning, I toss my jacket over the back of the brown sofa closest to the kitchen, looking beyond it to where Djinn now waits patiently on the coffee table. That book moves itself, and that bothers me.

"Wench."

I turn and face a glass held out to me. Stepping back to the counter, I take it, he clinks his glass to mine and we both down the contents. Putting my glass back on the white counter, I move to find music, when he grabs my elbow, pushing the shot glass back into my hand and refilling it.

"Three for luck," he explains.

He has a strange way of being instantly comfortable and reassuring, as if we've done this a hundred times before. I lick vanilla off my lip after the third dousing, moving back to the lounge, when he hooks my elbow again and spins me back.

"Would you stop running away and stand still for two bloody minutes."

Watching him from under my straight bangs poking at my eyes, he rummages through his jacket and unearths green. Four of them, already rolled.

I shake my head, "Too soon. I'll stick to my smokes."

"Where are they?"

I point at my jacket, and he hooks it with the toe of his Chuck Taylor, thanks to legs almost twice the length of mine. Flicking it, he catches it, handing it to me. Withdrawing the box of Marlboro, I offer him one. He takes one and lights both of ours before digging out cinnamon incense from his bag of tricks, lighting it, and moving away to stick it into the cork next to the sink.

Rapidly becoming spacey, I meander back to the lounge to put that music on, spotting the lavender smudge sticks in their jar next to the TV. Leaving The Doors to croon softly at us, Sasha wanders around lighting all the candles while I smog up the house with a bunch of lavender, simultaneously sucking on the filter of my smoke and adding to the ambiance with every exhalation.

I need to purify this place.

Blowing the flames out, I wave the smudge stick around over my head, walking toward the two bedrooms. He follows me, checking where the bathroom is and noting the study and bedroom, then the guest loo.

"You should do Burlesque."

Snapping my gaze back at him, I notice he's grabbed the twelve string guitar from my bedroom, "Why?"

"Your bedroom gives you away. I knew you had a hidden slut in you somewhere."

"Fuck off, Sasha. Is that why you're here? To snoop through everything?"

"Only your drawers dear."

Laughing, I keep wafting the smoking bunch of lavender around, "The lacy and satin drawers no doubt."

"Bet you go out in corsets too, don't you?"

"Bet you'd love to fuel your fantasies, who am I to shatter the dreams of a poet?" I volley back.

Settling in the lounge, he crushes the smudge stick out for me in the huge black bowl of sand I use as an ashtray. Pausing above it, he moves curious eyes over my face, "There's frankincense in here."

"Yeah, so?"

Djinn

"Just saying."

He moves back to the kitchen, collecting the empty glasses and vodka bottle, bringing them back to us where we sit opposite each other across a table with Djinn poised on the edge.

Refilling the glasses, we clink them together over the bowl.

"To getting to know each other."

I incline my head in response before chasing it down.

I crinkle my eyes against the smoke, "Have you eaten? I haven't. We could order in."

He swaps the Vanillia for Hot Monkey Pepper flavored vodka.

Tapping it, he grins at me, "Let's order Indian. I'm in the mood for blistering hot."

"Gah, you do love the innuendo. What about Thai? We can order take-out from Mai Thai and have it delivered?"

"Yeah, okay. Do you know what you want?" he asks, already thumbing through his phone for the number.

"Panang chicken curry, Andamun fried rice and Papaya Pok Pok salad."

"Nice choice. I knew I liked you. I'll add Goong Sarong and have the same."

I wait while he places the order, leaning back against the leather couch matching the one he's against, watching him shove long elegant fingers through unruly straight hair, talking on the phone, then gesturing as if the guy can see him when he gives the address.

Dropping his phone on the seat behind his head, he faces me, "So, tell me what happened with you and Djinn."

"It said I failed and then asked for you."

He arches his long neck and laughs, before engaging my gaze again, still looking bemused. "Seriously, what happened?"

"I'm not kidding. It rejected me." I shove the book his way and pick up the smokes again while he pours us spicy vodka, "I kid you not. Open it and read it for yourself."

He downs his shot before stealing my newly lit smoke, flicking Djinn open and leafing through the first pages.

Moving onto my knees to kneel for better leverage, I light another smoke and stare at the pages. This is impossible. It's completely different.

"Three hundred and sixty-six days of answers." He flips the page, "The man of your dreams is in your living-room, it's time to grab destiny by the balls."

Flicking my ash, I give him a sarcastic glare.

He pushes Djinn to me, downing his vodka and slamming the glass on the glossed wood of the sleeper table, "Not so scary. My instincts are telling me you couldn't wait for Saturday."

I stare at the open page which says; In 366 days your life will be transformed, starting today. Today wear purple and work on your breathing. Now ask the question.

It has a long gap and at the bottom reads; The answer to your question is; *Now is the time. No longer time to be afraid. Fate is for the questing, not the complacent. The future is here, and you own it.*

I snap the book closed, then open it again. It still looks the same.

Shaking my head, I sit back, "That's not possible."

"That's the very same book I gave to you."

"But it's not the book I read when I got home."

He grins, "Yet you probably took some potent self-medication when you got home, which you forgot to mention, right?"

"Nope."

"Someone laced your face powder with cocaine, you were overtired, and imagining things?"

"Scoff all you want, I know what I read. I'm jinxed I tell you. A book is making me look like I have a precarious grasp on reality, when I'm telling you the God's honest truth."

Djinn

Snuffing his smoke out, he stares at me for a long time in silence. Shrugging wide shoulders as if prepared to believe me, he digs in his jacket pocket and pulls out a leather bag.

Jiggling it to shuffle the order of the contents, he opens it, "Take one."

I put my hand in and withdraw a rune. The black stone is engraved with a white YV.

"You've drawn wild oxen. It means, 'Strength to be tamed', and adulthood. The tree it relates to is the birch, and is equal to the High Priestess card in tarot."

"So?"

"So, I believe you. You made Djinn behave the way it did. It's you that needs taming."

"Every second word out of your mouth sounds sexual."

He leans forward, glossy hair flopping into his eyes, "You're the untapped spirit. You don't know your own strength, but I can see it." Digging into the bag he brought with him which housed enough alcohol for a gathering, he pulls out a deck of cards and drops them loudly on the table. "Shuffle, cut, then draw the top card."

I'm beginning to feel mildly sleepy. The CD's shuffled over to Led Zeppelin; partial wailing swaths the air between us.

I do as bid, then hand them back without drawing a card.

He flips six cards over in a row in front of him. The Hierophant is first. He taps it with his pointer finger.

"Ritual and routine, religious guidance and authority, education in its formal sense. A seeker after knowledge and wisdom. Good sound advice, teaching and constructive counsel. Marriage, partnerships and morality."

He taps the next card, "King of Wands. A charming, responsible, loyal, entertaining, witty, honest, conscientious and generous person. A lover of the home and family life. A very passionate and virile man who is good at moral support and encouragement. When pushed or provoked he acts without hesitation, but can sometimes find this hard as he can often see both sides of an argument."

His grin leaves me in no doubt that the card in question refers to him.

He taps the next card. "The Lovers. Harmony and union, choices to be made using **intuition** and not intellect. Difficult decisions to be made not necessarily about love. Some form of test and consideration about commitments. Abstract thought, internal harmony and union, second sight. Possibly a struggle between two paths."

"You probably cheat at poker too, huh? Was that card up your sleeve? The lovers? Really?"

He shakes his head, pointing at it insistently.

The gaze he's giving me incinerates into my nervous system, "You have to make a choice, but at least you have a good friend willing to support you through it." He smiles but his eyes are unreadable. Looking at the next card he continues, "The Devil. Security versus creative or spiritual fulfillment. The High Priestess, again. This time reversed. Which means; lack of personal harmony and problems resulting from a lack of foresight. Suppression of the feminine or intuitive side of the personality. Facile and surface knowledge. Repression and ignorance of true facts and feelings. In women, an inability to come to terms with other women or themselves. Things and circumstances are not what they seem."

His free hand snakes across the table and covers mine as if to offer comfort.

"And finally, The Moon. Most auspicious considering it's a full moon tonight, and a blue one at that." He winks at me, "A bit like my balls."

This elicits a wry smile from me.

He sits forward to expound, "Imagination. Dreams and

Djinn

psychic impressions. Sometimes psychic work. Illusions. Inability to see things clearly sometimes resulting in personal depression. Losing control of one's daily life. The unconscious mind."

He releases my hand and refills our glasses, leaning back and surveying me over the rim of his before swallowing it all.

"Cinders, the only thing standing in the way of your happiness, is you. You have everything you require, including me, yet you deny it all as if it weren't pertinent."

To emphasize this point, Djinn heaves off the table and into my lap.

Ominous intuition snakes through my chakras while I suspiciously stare down at the supernatural book. The glass in my instantly numb fingers clatters to the table, forcing him to rescue his precious cards.

The room is spinning, gyrating wildly; this book unravels my grasp on reality.

"Well, if that isn't karmic confirmation the book is meant for you, I don't know what is."

He's chatting as if nothing weird just happened, retrieving the cloth from the kitchen to mop up my mess.

Halfway through wiping the table, the doorbell rings, and he shoves the cloth into my hand to complete the task to free him to answer the door.

I can't think, can't function, this book is burning a hole through my legs and I'm too afraid to touch it.

"Grubs up," filters to me from the other side of the galaxy.

An unholy ripping wakes me. Sitting up in bed, the distinct sound of glass breaking knifes fear down my spine. Wide awake, a shadow looms up next to me, washing me with cold trepidation.

"Jesus!"

Poppet

"No, just Sasha. What the fuck made that noise?"

It's pitch dark, the moon must have gone down early and in its stead is impenetrable blackness.

"Sounded like glass breaking."

"Where the hell is the light?"

I clap, shattering the frigid silence with the warm pink glow from my bedside lamp.

The details are hazy, probably because we depleted his green supply along with two bottles of vodka. He has no compunction and flips back the velvet quilt, holding a hand out to me to trail with him into the lounge, both as naked as a Sphinx. Diving out of bed, afraid to be alone, I walk with him to the threshold, gripping his hand with mine.

Terror shakes me, in turn I shake him and point to the mirror on the wall, completely cracked without any of the glass falling from the frame. His eyes are alert, slipping over me, he smiles despite the situation, tugging me into the darkness, one hand fumbling along the wall for the light switch.

He pitches head first into the darkness.

"Fuck." Finding the switch, I flip it. Djinn lies open on the floor between us, him sitting on the carpet rubbing his toes.

Staring at the possessed book which sits outside the bedroom like a welcome mat, I read the bold text.

I can help you, but you have to let me.

My finger is trembling along with my voice as I tell Sasha, "See, the book talks to me."

He nods, serious, "You are the chosen guardian."

A scuffling noise comes from the black hole around the corner from the passage, emanating from the lounge. He looks at me, eyebrows disappearing behind messy hair, eyes wide.

Something is clattering loudly, frenetic, urgent. And it's in *my* lounge.

"Oh God."

Djinn

 Chapter 4

Cindy:

Gripping Sasha's arm, we sneak slowly around the corner. With the light on, we look at the Ouija board with the planchette going ballistic across the wood.

It's got Tourette's syndrome with frenetic and urgent tics.

It's never done this before.

Crap.

I'm frightened of it, and stay behind the couch, in case.

"Get pen and paper," he orders me, moving across to the board and sitting on the chair in front of it, completely unselfconscious in his birthday suit.

Snatching up my notepad and pen from the microwave, I go and sit behind him, using him as a shield. It's clattering to the same letters over and over.

"O – N – T," he dictates. "D – O – I – T – D."

He repeats the same letters. Scrunching my eyes up I stare at them, forcing myself to concentrate.

"Don't do it." I look at him, gripping his knees with whitened fingers. "That's what it's saying."

"Don't do what?"

The planchette launches into the mirror opposite the couches hanging on the wall in a tortoiseshell frame, shattering it. Broken bits propel, pelting the couch.

Poppet

Sasha leaps up defensively, facing the wall.

His gray eyes look smoky in this light as he looks down at me with both eyebrows raised. "It's mightily pissed off."

"And I have to pee."

Afraid to go alone, I force myself to stand on unsteady legs and walk back to the passage with the bathroom. I halt on the threshold, staring at the mirror shards all over the floor. "Don't walk in here without shoes," I call back to him.

Changing my mind, I go to the guest toilet. There's no mirror in there. By the time I exit, a familiar song is breaking the oppressive silence, and not in a good way.

"Did you have to choose the song singing about fuck god?"

"Why not? When in doubt, get cheeky."

I nod, making my way back to the bedroom to pull on a gown. He keeps staring at my bits and it's bothering me as I don't really remember what the hell happened between us. The kettle heating filters into the room while I wrap myself in a red kimono.

"You're one hot babe."

Before I can turn, his arms straitjacket me and he kisses my neck like a familiar lover. His stubble is as abrasive as rubbing a sea urchin down my neck, leaving a hot rash in its wake.

"So when are we going to the Jolly Roger?" he asks.

"Why?"

"Happy hour's from four to seven. Let's go this week."

"For grub and grog, or just grog?"

"Both."

Maybe he has ADD because I have no idea how anyone can change the subject that smoothly.

"Yeah, we'll go. But first let's clean up the glass."

He moves back to the doorway and hefts Djinn into his arms, staring at the open page with the bold lettering.

"You haven't answered it."

"I'm not ready to."

Djinn

"Why not?"

"The board told me not to."

He sits on the edge of the bed, watching me in silence as I slip on flip-flops and make my way to the kitchen to get the dustpan and brush. My stomach is quaking worse than a supernova exploding and all I want to do is run.

My life's turned upside down, and it started with that book.

"Why did you give me Djinn?" I ask, as we sip coffee twenty minutes later.

"It felt right. I have a good feeling about it."

My nerves are on edge and for once I'm glad to have company.

I'm skittish when he leans over to plant a hand on my leg, "Do you want to stay at my place for the rest of the night?"

I nod fervently, ready to leave in my kimono right this second. "I'll call in sick for work. I'm going to be wasted tomorrow."

"In that case, let's get wasted."

"I thought we did?"

He has a rogue smile which sits slightly skew across his face, making him instantly attractive, "Then let's do it again."

Do it? I'm not going to ask.

"Let's wait until we get to your place," I say, playing it safe, unsure if I should read innuendo into his statement or not.

He nods, placing his empty mug on the table in front of us in the lounge. The second he releases the handle it turns into a trajectory, smashing into the same mirror.

"Fuck you! That'd better be cleaned up by the time I get home!" I yell into the hollow silence.

I'm losing it. I'm holding on, barely. If I didn't have him here I'd be locked in the bedroom closet with the rosary I wear as a necklace.

In fact, I think I'm going to wear it right now.

Poppet

Standing, I begin marching to the bedroom to get clothes on, "Let's go."

Sasha:

While we get dressed, the guitar starts strumming in the lounge. Cindy stops, one leg in black jeans, the other balancing her. She falters, looking close to tears.

"Does shit like this normally happen in your home?"

"No," she snaps at me, turning to pull a rosary over her head.

She fluffs out her short fine hair, glancing my way before pulling a tank top on. Her eyes are still rimmed in dark kohl, making her pallid face look like a mortician's experiment. She stuffs essentials into a bag and rushes at me, holding my hand with the grip of a woman holding the lid off her coffin while someone nails it shut. I nod encouragement, determined not to let her see how unnerved her poltergeist is making me.

Pausing in the lounge, we stuff the alcohol and other personal items into our bags, she picks up her purse, and we head for the door.

"Leave the lights on," she tells me.

An almighty smack to the back of my head smashes my nose into the front door. Stunned, I wait for my vision to clear.

"Fucking book."

She bends down to pick it up, and as she does the double couch barrels across the floor at her head. Catching her shoulder just in time, I haul her upright and against the door.

"Jesus."

She's shaken, the Jesus she uttered is muffled by the thump of the furniture into the wall behind where she was just leaning over.

Not waiting another second, I snatch the door open and shove her through it, slamming it closed behind us.

She clamps my hand into hers and we begin running for the

Djinn

stairs.

I'm relieved to be home. After guiding her upstairs and pouring us both a triple hazelnut vodka, we sit smoking, staring at each other from opposite sides of the bed.

"What did the book say?"

She flicks her ash into the large shell ashtray in the middle between us, then looks at me with pursed lips.

"Choose."

"Djinn said choose?"

"Yup."

"Choose what? None of this makes sense."

"Djinn wants me to choose to interact with him, but the Ouija board definitely said not to."

"Why didn't you warn me you have a poltergeist?"

"I didn't have a poltergeist. My home was my sanctuary until I took Djinn in there."

"Are you saying this is my fault?"

"No, I'm saying it's either Djinn, or Djinn has woken a latent energy in my home and it started tonight."

"How bad is my nose?"

She laughs softly, "You look fine, promise." Then her expression sobers, "Thanks for rescuing me from the couch."

"Fuck this."

Putting the glasses and ashtray on the floor, I grab her, pulling her under me so I can stare into her eyes.

It's like coming back from war, every fiber of your being simply craves the act of confirming life. She seems to have the same idea as hands grips into my hair and she yanks my face down to hers.

Poppet

Cindy:

Blissfully happy, floating, I am buoyed as if in water. Staring up into the perfect sky, clouds scud, birds twitter, and somewhere at a distance, children giggle.

Turning my head, I spy Sasha smiling at me.

We laugh together with some secret I can't remember.

The sunshine snuffs instantaneously as the serenity is sliced with a murderous scream. An endless wail of torture.

My eyes snap open and I sit up, but the screaming doesn't stop. God, it sounds like someone is being burned alive, it's beginning to gurgle now, a gargled wet roar of pain.

The light flicks on and Sasha sits up, pushing his hair off his forehead and staggering across to the window to look out.

"Some idiot hit the street lamp."

Turning, he fumbles in discarded jeans for his cell phone. The tone is familiar when he presses 911.

This night is never going to end. When will the sun come up? How many times have we tried to go to sleep just to be woken with calamity.

He slips into jeans and shoes, naked from the hips up, "You coming?"

"Yup."

Hauling my ass out of his warm bed, I slip my own jeans and jumper on, then step into my shoes. I'm too afraid to be left alone.

Thundering down the stairs together, he races for the front door, flinging it open and bounding with those long legs into the street. He goes around to the driver's window to check on the lady while I catch up. Lights have come on across the road.

"He was just standing there like the grim reaper. Only after I hit him did I see his face. Such a beautiful young man. Is he alive? Oh God, he's dead isn't he? Isn't **he**? He's dead. He's dead. Oh God. God, I killed a man ..."

Djinn

Sasha gives me a frustrated glance over the roof of the car, "Ma'am, please calm down. There's no one else here but you. We called 911 –"

"I killed him. **I killed him**. Don't just stand there boy. Look under the wheels. I have to know. Tell me. I killed him, didn't I? Oh God, I killed a boy your age. Oh God. Oh God. Oh..."

Dropping to my haunches, I look under her car. There's nothing there.

"Please ma'am, you're bleeding profusely, please sit still–"

"I killed a boy!" she hollers like a banshee. It screeches enough to pour goose-bumps down my back.

There's something just in front of the headlights. One of them is pointing down instead of forward. Standing, I walk to the front of her car. It smells terrible, as if she ruptured the radiator when she hit the pole and knocked the lid off a spiritual sewer simultaneously.

The night spirals, her headlights dance up and down and spin, dropping to my knees, I bury my nose between them to stop myself from fainting.

"Cindy?!" Sasha shouts. "Hold on ma'am, I'll be right back."

A hand holds my shoulder as warmth wraps around me, "Babes? You okay?"

I shake my head, daring to lift the weight on my neck to look at him, tears unchecked now, and point under the bumper, "Djinn."

His head whips like Emily Rose being exorcised. The hand on my shoulder trembles as he leans forward, blocking out the beam from the headlight, dragging the book out and hefting it into his left hand.

"You keep it. It told me it wanted to be returned to Para-Dice."

The wailing of sirens competes with the hysterical wailing from the woman in the VW.

Poppet

We look at each other, lost for words. With the light full in his face, he looks as haunted as I feel.

My teeth rattle loudly in my mouth against each other like sugar cubes in an empty cup.

⛧

Djinn

Chapter 5

Cindy:

Staring up at the faint lamp light filtering through navy curtains from the street, I'm listening, trying to figure out what woke me. Third time lucky eh?

Creak.

What was that?

I'm tempted to put my hand over Sasha's mouth and nose to shut his deep breathing up so I can hear.

Creak.

Oh God. That was right here.

Lifting slowly, propped on my elbow, I peer at the darkness at the end of the king sized bed. My eyes haven't adjusted and I can't see anything.

Clunk.

Terrified, I can't move, can't breathe, can't see. This is almost as delightful as sleep paralysis with Hannibal in the room.

Opposite the bed, a flame bursts into life and the white candle spreads an eerie glow over the wall and ceiling. The corners deepen with shadows.

Creak.

It's the floor. The floor is creaking as if someone is walking around; in here.

"Who's there?" I whisper.

Poppet

Whirring flick-flacks as the book on the drawers thumps open, banging the wood with an abrupt and insistent knock. The candle's flame wavers hysterically while pages turn in an endless arc. They stop as suddenly as they began.

In disbelief, I stare at the candle behind the book, highlighting a face hovering above the open pages, between me and the wall, watching, waiting.

Floating higher, the flame illuminates an eye, an ethereal and ghostly eye of startling blue.

Squeezing my eyes shut, I open them again. The face looks like a skull now. It morphs constantly between subliminally beautiful and grotesque.

"Djinn?"

It blinks, the mouth curves into a grin, it bobs a nod.

"What do you want?"

I'm too afraid to get out of bed and go over there.

The pages snap impatiently. White mist lifts slowly from the book, shrouding the wall in luminescent white.

HELP.

It's black in the white mist, impossible to ignore.

"Why?"

SAVE ME.

My intestines lurch like a ship's rope caught by the anchor when I carefully lift the duvet and step onto the floor.

Creak.

Nearly giving myself cardiac arrest with the floor giving under my weight, I whip about, looking for an intruder behind me with a plastic bag ready to stuff over my head.

Thump.

The book judders on the drawers to draw my attention back.

Swallowing compulsively, I inch slowly forward, eyes riveted to the face floating above the pages.

Keeping my distance, I peer at the blank page with a foot

Djinn

between us.

I can't protect you from them, from in here.

"Who's them?"

Demons.

"What demons?"

In your home, in your life, in your car, at your work.

"They want you, not me. You wanted to return to Sasha, so stop complaining."

Where did that come from? All I want is to be rescued.

Why don't I trust this book?

Djinn lifts and drops heavily back onto the dresser.

CLUNK.

Sasha rolls and groans in his sleep.

Staring at the mirage, I dare to ask, "Are you Djinn?"

The spectral face with the blue eyes nods.

Scratching scuffles the paper and new writing appears.

You are my destiny. Help me and I will help you.

"How do I help you?"

Choose.

"I can't, not yet."

You don't have time. They're coming.

"Who's coming?"

Them.

As I read the words, the bedroom door slams closed behind me, the candle snuffs out, the book thunks closed, and Sasha bolts out of bed in one fluid movement.

"What the fuck was that?" he says.

His voice is husky, but after the candlelight I'm plunged back into blindness.

"Cindy? Is that you?"

I can't answer, something has my larynx and is squeezing the breath from me. Pulled backward, pounded against the wall, my head knocks with each thrust as I'm forced up the plaster.

Poppet

Clawing at my throat, there's nothing there.
BANG.
Oh god.
"Fuck!" comes from the darkness.
Sasha makes noises like he walked into something and hurt himself. My vision is becoming white, spotted with red dots like hemorrhaging droplets of burst blood vessels ...
Click.
The light is on, I just see it before my vision clouds completely.
Rattled like a doll held by a Parkinson's patient, I'm aware I'm hanging above the room before fainting.

Sasha:

"Jesus!"
Cindy flings up the wall, her head knocking it like a spirit wanting entrance, then stiff as a mirror she hangs on the ceiling, her eyes rolled back and tongue protruding.
Flicking my gaze erratically, I'm still trying to figure out what woke me first. Fear licks my skin with icy saliva.
"Cindy!"
Bounding onto the bed, I bounce off the mattress to grab her ankle, catching it and pulling her feet first back to the bed, my knees give on the unsteady mattress and I lose my balance, but manage to hold onto her. Like a mannequin filled with helium she wants to buoy upward, retaining rigor mortis rigidity.
She's like a scarecrow buffeted by a hurricane as she flays, jerking maniacally as if trying to pull free.
Djinn slaps open, pages fanning furiously, calling me, but I can't let her go. I daren't.
"Let go!"
Nothing happens.

Djinn

Whatever has her isn't giving up that easy.
Book - Cindy? Book – Cindy – Book ...
Book.

Releasing her ankle, she hinges woodenly, slamming both heels into the ceiling-board, face down, looking at the floor below sightlessly. Flying across the room, I snatch up the book and run back to the bed, standing on it again and leaping to snare her back. Each time my hand comes close, she shoots further away. As if to emphasize who is in control here, she dips halfway between the floor and ceiling before being flung back at the roof with a skull cracking CLONK.

Dropping Djinn on the rumpled bed, I stage dive for her feet, both of us dropping to the floor. Her head connects with the disused amp in the corner while my knee explodes with agony. Trying to bury my alarm, I watch blood trickle from where she bit her tongue with the impact, and the blood on the floor behind shocking white hair.

Dragging her with me back to the bed, one arm tight around her waist, I haul us both back onto the bed and stare at the open pages.

NOW! NO TIME.

She yanks; I scratch her thigh in my mad scrambling to regain a hold on her body. Shaking uncontrollably, her eyes open, unseeing pupils stare at me.

"Evil man. Evil man. You **evil** man."

I almost release my hold in repulsion as a twisted abrasive voice emanates from her throat.

She points at the book, "Burn it. **Burn it!** BURN IT!"

The stiffness releases her body and she crumples on top of Djinn, smearing blood across the page. The bedroom door swings wide and whams the door handle into the wall, ricocheting back in unholy warbles.

"Oh Jesus."

Poppet

Cindy's eyes clear and she stares up at me, confusion and tears intermingling, "What's going on?"

As the words leave her mouth the bed becomes the possessed. Rebounding off the floorboards like a gymnast on the springboard, we bounce into the centre of the room, clinging to each other, sprawled on an ancient book, the foundation of our reality gyrates wildly along with the bed.

Bucking, trying to fling us, I have my arms stretched wide, holding her down underneath me while gripping the bed frame on either side. Her eyes shut while slender arms tourniquet around my neck; fighting nausea, I wait it out with my eyes closed.

We halt. Her breathing is ragged in my ear, her body trembling under me; somehow this wasn't how I pictured this scenario.

Opening my eyes, I wait.

All is calm. The room immediately degrees warmer.

Slowly letting her go, we sit up, on knees, gripping hands, too afraid to speak, to move, to challenge.

POP.

The bulb in the lamp explodes just as Djinn levitates off the duvet.

⛧

Djinn

 Chapter 6

Sasha:

Gripping her hands, I pull her with me, "We have to get out of here."

"Okay," whispers shakily.

Her hands clutching mine betray fear.

"Where are your clothes?" I ask, distracting myself with action.

"I can't see anything."

Releasing her fingers I walk from memory to the curtains, yanking them open to unveil streetlight. After the darkness, it's easy to navigate.

"Just grab your clothes, don't bother putting them on," I order.

My keys and wallet are still in my jeans; where the hell is my phone?

"Do you have your phone on you?"

"Yes, in my jeans," she says.

With an armful of clothes, I make my way around to her side. Holding her elbow I guide her with me to the door, and by sheer fluke catch a glimpse of my phone on the bed. Leaning over, I snatch it as if Djinn will bite me, reclaiming her arm and thrusting her across the threshold before we get locked in.

"Move, just hightail it."

Thundering barefoot down the stairs, I'm elated when the

Poppet

door opens and we're allowed out into the yard.

Doing a quick survey, I hide her behind me as we move across the lawn to the waiting Honda.

"We're alone. I'll just pull my jeans on, you can get dressed in the car."

Her white hair radiates the artificial light like a birthday candle on sugar. It's a moment which returns humanity. Opening the vehicle with the remote, I take the opportunity to pull her quaking body for a hug, squeezing and inhaling unique perfume; it's so familiar.

She scrambles into the back, immediately yanking on clothes; chucking mine onto the passenger seat, I pull on jeans and get behind the wheel.

Thank God it starts. Pulling off like a moron, I nail the accelerator to the floorboard. It's times like this I'm grateful the CR-Z does nought to a hundred in ten seconds.

"Where are we going?"

Dressed, she slithers her way between the seats while I drive us away down SE Hawthorne boulevard.

"Holy ground."

"Pull over, I'll drive while you get dressed."

"Not stopping. Not for anything, or anyone."

It takes less than five minutes at this hour for us to reach Lone Fir Cemetery on 26th Avenue. Parking in the street outside the perimeter, I open my door, using the leg room to lace up my Chuck Taylor's.

"Why here?"

"It's the oldest cemetery in the neighborhood. It was founded in 1846, so it should be hallowed ground."

Standing, I reach back in to grab my shirt and jacket. She watches me with big eyes, staying silent while I dress.

"Open the glove compartment," I instruct.

"Why?"

Djinn

"Smokes."

At last, a smile. It's weak, but it's still a smile.

Escorting her from the car, we walk in the brisk predawn air to the wrought iron fence. Helping Cindy over, I feel delivered jumping down after her onto cherished land.

Sitting down under a stand of trees I light us each a smoke, inhaling deeply, pleased my hands do not shake like the one rubbing my leg.

Looking down at the rebel blond, I ask softly, "Are you okay?"

She nods, not looking up but staring fixedly at my thigh, biting her lip. Giving her time to regain composure, I slump against the bark of the tree, smoking, covering the hand on my leg with my own and squeezing it.

"It's going to be okay."

"How can you even say that? My life has turned to shit."

She's looking at me. Ghostly light catches the moisture on her lashes like winter rime.

"Correction, that would be *our* lives, not your life alone." I wish I could comfort her, but she messed with my sanity when bouncing off the ceiling and talking like a possessed puppet.

Is she the problem, or is it really Djinn? Or something else entirely?

"What the hell happened back there?"

I don't have the heart to tell her. "It's freaky shit, but there are solutions for this sort of problem."

"Like what?"

"The Phantom Professionals."

"Do you think we're being haunted?"

"I don't know what this is, all I know is I'm not equipped to handle it."

"The smudging didn't work. I thought it was supposed to purify a house of evil."

Poppet

"Cinders, I don't know what we're dealing with. Smudging doesn't always work. Maybe we need a priest?"

"My cards yesterday said I was about to receive 'protection and power'. But then at church, La Comtesse de la Nuit told me to choose, or I would burn."

"Well, she's just full of shit. I don't know why you waste your time there. She's too good for the masses, have you noticed? Self ordained hypocrite."

"What's your problem?"

"Cin, if you want a message from the dead giving you guidance, you don't need a madwoman to be an intermediary. We could hold a séance and get answers ourselves."

"I don't think I can handle that idea after tonight."

"You drew the High Priestess, twice. Things and circumstances are not what they seem."

"Sasha, the bed was having an epileptic fit. I don't see how that can be interpreted any other way."

I check my phone. It's 4:46. Too early to call for help. "God, I'm tired. But way too wired to sleep."

Her answer is to snuggle up to me, leaning her head on my chest, one hand hugging the inside of my thigh.

"You're the only good thing that happened last night," I reassure into her hair.

"Bet you're sorry you wanted a date with me now, huh?"

There's humor in her voice. A small slice of normality.

Impulsively I move hair off her face and tuck it behind her ear, "You're going to get through this."

If anything, I should be thanking Djinn. I've waited years to get this close to her, and overnight the playing field has changed and I'm getting high scores. I even stepped up to bat a few times but backed down, resistant to pushing her too far, too soon.

Looking up at the dawn streaked sky, I'm exactly where I want to be. Cindy's cuddled up against me, holding my hand.

Djinn

We're in this together to the end. I couldn't have executed this better if I'd planned it. Djinn is my blessing, even if it's her curse. In a few hours every boundary she built up has been crushed with biblical ease. Although, I doubt I'll have another erection looking at her. Every time I do, the unseeing woman in her body takes over and shuts my own down with cold fishhooks plucking at my soul.

I can get over this, I have to.

Instead, I rub a hand absently over my nape, hoping it's not her, it's the book.

How is it that women keep such a diverse inventory of sundry items in their purses? Thanks to antibacterial wipes, there's no longer blood in her hair, or on her face.

At seven, I drive us over to NE Multnomah Street through wonderfully normal morning traffic, directly to McDonald's for breakfast.

The irony of driving down Martin Luther King Jr boulevard, isn't lost on me. I had a dream. I had a dream of landing this cute babe, and when I get close enough to cuddle in the same bed, all hell breaks loose.

After a brief discussion with her, I leave her at our table and go order three bacon, egg, and cheese, McGriddles, two for me and one for her, and a plate of hotcakes with our McCafé lattés.

Returning, I slide into my chair and stare at blue eyes smudged with charcoal smiles.

"How much sleep did you get last night?" I ask her, handing over food and drink.

"I haven't a clue, but I have a headache from hell."

"Yeah, you have dark rings under your eyes."

"You?"

Unleashing a rascal grin, I say, "If it was up to me you

wouldn't have slept at all."

"How is it that guys can think of sex when they've just had a night of utter Purgatory?"

"We're easily side-tracked."

"Oh? How did you get side-tracked?"

Shooting her a brief wink, I reveal, "You're cold. It made me think of more enjoyable things than hiding in a cemetery."

She folds her arms, fumbling, caught between wanting to drink her coffee and exposing her chest under its thin pullover, or staying with her arms folded.

Her grin is wry, "I get cold when I'm tired."

"Your coffee will warm you up. Or you could sit next to me and huddle," I'm smiling now.

She picks up her coffee and continues to sip it, hunching her shoulders as if against a cold draught. We eat in silence for some time before I intrude on her festering thoughts.

"Tell me about yourself. Despite knowing you for three years, I don't know much about the real Cindy."

"What do you want to know?"

"Everything. It looks like we're in this together, and I'd like to get to know my cell mate a little better."

"I'm twenty-four, single obviously, love where I work but hate the job and the people, um ..."

"Where do you work?"

"Central Library."

"Oh cool. Yeah, that makes perfect sense for you."

"What about you?" she redirects at me.

"A year older than you, handsome, charming, great to cuddle, wicked smile, and a magnificent chef."

She laughs indulgently; dang it's good to hear her laugh without pretense.

"I forgot to mention self-employed and a proprietor of a business which is your weakness. Admit it, we're made for each

Djinn

other." I give her a wink.

Her face loses congeniality and she stares moodily out the window.

Reaching across, I comfort her hand, "What is it?"

She shakes her head, determinedly averting her gaze. Mild anxiety tightens to harp string tension.

We sit like that for at least a minute, before she meets my gaze. "I've lost too much. Djinn is undoing the little I have left."

I answer with a questioning frown.

"My folks had me late. A few years ago my dad was diagnosed with Alzheimer's. I'd call it dementia. He left the gas on and burnt the house down, with him and mom both in it."

Tears trickle and drip off her lashes when she looks down, now squeezing my hand back. "How do you think I found the money to start Para-Dice?" She shakes her head and shrugs, her mouth twisting unattractively. "My dad always wanted to learn to fly. He finally got his license, took mom up for a show off flight, and ran out of fuel. We have more in common than you think."

"Can we go?" she whispers.

I nod, scooping our meal off the table and leading her back to the car with an arm around her shoulders.

The moment she's back in the privacy of the CR-Z, she bursts into tears, hugging me like a pedestrian to a street pole in a gale. I wait it out, comforting her, letting her excavate tissues from her purse to blow her nose and dry eyes.

"Cindy, this all happened for a reason. The last thing I'm going to do is let supernatural shit mess up perfection. Let's call the exterminators, get rid of the problem, and get back to having fun."

She nods, a grim smile the only offering.

# Chapter 7

Sasha:

Looking out the window, I wait for the ringing to stop.

"You have reached the Phantom Professionals. We specialize in exterminating paranormal predators. How can I help you?"

"Yeah hi. Um, do you do immediate call outs?"

"Yes we do. What is the nature of the activity?"

"Mostly behaving like a poltergeist. Mirrors breaking, furniture moving, doors slamming ..."

Shit, I should have had this conversation in private. I need to be able to tell her about Cindy becoming a kite.

"Who am I speaking to?"

"Sasha Lewis."

"Sasha, you're speaking to Heather. When did this activity start?"

"Last night. And it followed us from my friend's house to my own. We spent the rest of the night hiding in a cemetery. I was hoping you could sort out the problem this morning so we can go home."

"Okay Sasha. Let me just have a word with Graham. In the meantime what is your address and phone number?"

I give her both and wait.

"We can meet you there in ten minutes. Is there anything else we should know?"

Djinn

"Yes, but I'll wait to talk to you about it in person."

"I understand. Thank you for contacting the Phantom Professionals. We'll meet you shortly."

"Bye."

I check the time on my phone.

"Why did you give her my address?"

My attention diverts back to the withdrawn vixen in the passenger seat, "I figured you'd like to get to go home first."

"Oh."

But a smile of relief cracks her tense mask, and I offer a wink in reply. Starting the engine, we make our way back to SE 37th Ave and Market.

Sasha:

"So nothing out of the ordinary. No ectoplasm, taps turning on and off, walls oozing ghastly substances, no odd smells, being touched or thrown, being burnt, having your skin slashed open, none of the usual anomalies?" Heather says as if she is asking for a shopping list.

"The guitar started playing on its own, the mirrors cracked, the Ouija board got really excited and threw the planchette into the mirror in here, and the book, Djinn, kept hopping about and opening and closing on its own. If that doesn't qualify as out of the ordinary, I don't know what does," Cindy objects.

"Where is this book?"

"At my place," I say.

And what exactly happened at your place, and what is the address?"

"What is your preoccupation with addresses?"

"We have a paranormal map of the area. Certain locations receive more activity than others. We've found that all homes inside the paranormal triangle tend to become active over full moon, and it was a full moon last night. The homes located directly on the boundary line, particularly the points, have the most aggressive activity during the yearly cycles of equinox, solstice, and full moons."

"I'm down the road just before the corner of Hawthorne boulevard and SE 37th Avenue."

"And have you experienced paranormal activity in your home in the past?"

"No. Last night was the first time."

"What happened last night?"

Cindy speaks up, "The bed had a fit like it swallowed its tongue. The doors banged around, the light popped, Djinn lit a candle and spoke to me ..."

"I beg your pardon? A book spoke to you?"

"Yes."

"I think we're going to have to start with the book. And how did it speak to you?"

Heather and Graham exchange a glance which clearly says the only problem in this equation is Cindy's sanity.

After an hour of complete boredom and zero supernatural activity, we head over to my place. Deliberately I have Heather in my car, after convincing Cindy to travel with Graham, using the lame excuse of each of us with a professional is better than us being alone.

"I have to tell you something," I broach with Heather as I navigate the roads.

"Yes?"

"Cindy had something take hold over her last night, but she doesn't seem to remember."

"What happened exactly?"

"She juddered her way up the wall, hung from the ceiling,

Djinn

dipped and flung back, I caught her and held her down on the bed when she hinged up again and said in one fucked up voice, to burn the book. Then she collapsed and asked me what was happening."

"Sasha, have you considered the problem is neither of your homes, but Cindy herself? It's quite possible for people to cause paranormal activity, including manifesting blood on walls and turning appliances on and off. The subconscious mind is incredibly powerful."

Pulling in behind Graham's graphite Prius, I turn to the short redhead. "I've known her for years. Yes, she's intrigued with the occult, but she's not evil. She never has been. If she's the problem, then Djinn is the catalyst."

A knock on the window forces me to abandon the conversation. Getting out, I join my pale friend on the sidewalk.

After giving them the tour, I end up trailing Heather downstairs, around the store, while Cindy and Graham cover upstairs.

Her EMF reader only spikes around plugs and lights, and I'm finding the digital audio recordings quite amusing.

"I'm not here to hurt you, I'm here to communicate," Heather says.

This is followed with a forty second pause, during which time I scan the room with an infra-red scanner, to no avail.

"What made you so angry last night?"

Pause.

"Do you have a name? I'm Heather, this is Sasha. I'm sure you know Sasha already. What's your name?"

She's using a tone as if speaking to a toddler. I'm not sure condescending is the right approach, but what do I know?

Pause.

We're walking between the bookshelves now and she lingers

to stare at the mirror on the rear wall.

"How long has that mirror been there?" she asks, looking at me.

"Years and years. It's a family heirloom."

"I see. You do realise that mirrors are portals? Whoever broke the mirrors in Cindy's home did it to protect her. I would suggest you cover that or get rid of it."

"I'll cover it."

There's no way I'm getting rid of my grandma's mirror. I loved watching her put on pink lipstick before going out or answering the front door. She was adorably old fashioned that way. If anyone is in that mirror, it's someone who loves me dearly.

Picking up the sheet I use to cover valuables when I go on vacation, I move to the back of the store and shield it.

"Hello? Can you hear me?"

"I can hear you just fine," I answer automatically.

"I was talking to the presence, not you."

"Oh."

I shut up, shove my hands in my pockets, and continue trailing the exterminator.

"Is there something you need me to know?"

Pause.

"Thank you for your time. If you need me to come back and help you, just knock three times."

Immediately the ceiling above us resounds three times.

Like Lucifer's metronome, my heartbeat responds with ferocious pounding. It's like I've been punched in the throat, I can't breathe. Struggling to inhale, I ignore the sinister breath ghosting my nape.

"I'm right here. Tell me what you need. How can I help you?"

Pause.

"Okay, well give me an hour to process this recording and I'll get back to you. Thank you for trusting me and for your

Djinn

communication."

She looks at me through the dim lighting caused by the closed shutters, nods with tension compressing her mouth, and depresses the stop button.

Turning, I take the lead, going up the creaky Oregon pine steps to find the other two.

Graham wastes no time in securing Heather's arm in his hand when we arrive upstairs in the bedroom, leading her straight to Djinn.

"Look at this."

He holds the EMF detector over the book and all of the LED's light up.

"Did it speak to you?" she asks in a derisive tone.

"No. It's just a regular book."

At least he attempted to whisper his answer. My skin is still crawling from the three knocks on the ceiling.

Walking over to Cindy who's staring with a petulant expression out the window, I ask, "Did you guys hear a knock up here?"

"No."

She doesn't move, refusing to look at me.

"Why is there blood on this book?" Heather asks behind us.

She sounds alarmed, and that alarms me. Swiveling to face them, I explain, "It happened accidentally last night. Cindy knocked her head, so doesn't remember, but when I put her on the bed, she smeared blood on Djinn."

Heather looks directly at Cindy with a sharpness which betrays panic, "This is your blood?"

"I guess."

"Graham, let's go back to the car to listen to the recordings."

She looks at us, "Maybe you two can make coffee?"

"I apologise. I was so caught up in the drama I lost my manners. Coming right up." I offer a chastised smirk. Looking at

Poppet

Cinders, I ask, "You coming?"

She nods, latching onto my arm with her own.

Once we're alone in the kitchen, I turn to her while waiting for the water to boil, "What happened up there?"

"He's an asshole."

Her answer ignites my inner warrior.

"Why? What did he do?"

"They're blaming me for everything."

"They're just looking for logical explanations."

"No, they're not. They're looking for a quick resolution so they can charge you for their so called expertise."

"What did he say?"

"Djinn is a normal book steeped in energy from its ancient past. But I have unresolved issues, apparently, and I'm making this shit happen. So now they're fucking shrinks. He's a bloody idiot and I want them gone."

Pouring water into the mugs, I stir absently before looking at her.

"Let's wait to see what Heather says."

She folds her arms, narrows her eyes, and glares out the kitchen window, effectively ignoring me because I won't do as she asks.

Sitting around the lounge, I'm conscious of how bachelor and student looking my home is. These two are dressed as if they're from Texas and are on their way to church.

Sipping coffee, Heather presses play on her laptop.

"I'm not here to hurt you, I'm here to communicate."

Static scratches before a gruff distant voice hisses, "Go away."

She pauses it and looks at us.

"You two have a problem."

The hand on my leg tightens exponentially, and I cover it with

Djinn

my own.

"What made you so angry last night?"

"... No – help."

The abrasive male voice is saturated in malice. It gives me the creeps.

"Do you have a name? I'm Heather, this is Sasha. I'm sure you know Sasha already. What's your name?"

"Go away."

"Hello? Can you hear me?"

"Get out!"

"Is there something you need me to know?"

"Leave!"

"Thank you for your time. If you need me to come back and help you, just knock three times."

Immediately three hollow booms ring out, just as it happened. An eerie reverberation starts, like someone blowing into an empty bottle. It hollows out my soul and siphons the warmth from me. Giddy, I lean back and cradle my coffee, grateful for the heat. Unearthing my hand from Cindy's clinging grip, I pinch the bridge of my nose, freezing with the next hoarse words.

"I will kill you. **Get out!**"

She stops the playback when a tortured wail vibrates the speakers. The hollow bottle sound turned into wailing. A wailing that shreds everything sanctified inside you. My spirit was just flayed with evil whips dipped in lava and I fight the reflex to double over and vomit. I don't know how it's possible, but I feel violated.

"You have a presence, and it's not downstairs, it's upstairs."

I look at Heather and am desperate to tell her Cindy feels strongly about them getting out and leaving her alone.

Maybe it is Cin?

Graham speaks up, "Do you have somewhere you can stay for a few days?"

Poppet

"Why?" I ask.

My voice sounds numb and monotone, even to me.

"If we exorcise this place, it's going to get violent."

This announcement is followed with three consecutive bangs on the ceiling above us. Dust falls like black snow, clouding my perception and making me wish we could go back and start again. This isn't my home. Djinn was here for a week before Cindy stopped by.

It has to be her.

Looking at her, a shocked inhalation breaks the awkward silence when I notice her baleful glare directed at the Phantom Professionals.

BANG.

BANG – BANG.

Clearing my throat, doused in cold fear, I am paralyzed as I stare at them.

Djinn

 Chapter 8

Sasha:

Looking at Cindy, I give her arm a soft compressing squeeze, "Shall we go?"

She shakes her head, still glaring at Heather and Graham.

"You heard him. Get out! Before you unleash all hell into my life, I suggest you do exactly as you're told."

Graham leans forward, elbows on knees, "Cindy, I don't think you understand–"

"I understand perfectly. If you don't get out, your wife dies. Stay if you want to get rid of her, or leave if you love her. The choice is yours."

She gets up to dismiss them and end the discussion, stomping to the stairs and taking them with reverberating force.

I look at them apologetically. "I don't know what's wrong with her. I'm so sorry ..."

Heather interrupts, "She's bonded with it. Her blood was spilled last night. She needs help." Fear paints her face in bandage hues, "Now Sasha! Today!"

Cindy - or Djinn - must have heard, because Heather's eyes roll back while I'm staring at her, and she stands ironing board straight, floating off the floor.

I know I'm staring like a heretic on the torture rack with my eyeballs drying out, but I'm immobile with the terror roiling my

Poppet

gut.

Graham rockets out of his seat, gripping her while she levitates higher toward the ceiling where the knocks emanated.

"Don't just sit there man! Help me!"

My limbs react like chewing gum softened on pavement, they refuse to solidify and hold my weight.

Flopping about with effort, my knees fold on the attempt to stand, and I crawl around the coffee table to hold onto her. Grabbing an ankle, searing heat cracks down my arm like a static shock, impulsively I release my hold.

"Die. You're all going to die."

Her chain-saw statement is enough to catapult Graham into grabbing her and running for the front door, flinging it wide and running out into the yard with her, where she collapses like a used condom.

Her voice was exactly the tone of a whining chain-saw cutting through a knot.

Where's Cindy?

This pumps strength to vital organs because I start running before I'm fully aware I'm going up the stairs.

"Cindy!"

I halt in the bedroom doorway as she snatches Djinn off the dresser.

"I can't take another second of this, Sasha."

Cindy:

Grabbing Djinn, flicking it open to a blank page, I hiss with desperation, "If I say yes, will this shit stop?"

Yes.

"How can I be certain?"

It only came to prevent you from owning your power. Fear is a great motivator.

Djinn

"What caused all of," I pause, gesturing at the world around me to encompass the everything that's recently happened, "this?'

Evil exists. You are about to become powerful. It is the nature of evil to turn the righteous from the path of their enlightenment. The energy is everywhere, today it was your turn to experience it.

"Why?"

If you choose me, you become their enemy. That was to be prevented at all costs. Once you unleash the power I will share with you, they can no longer have the upper hand. They don't wish for you to become powerful. They seek to incriminate me, yet you left me alone to fend for myself.

Jeez. This book is giving me a guilt trip. What the heck?

Sasha:

She's delicate, gorgeous, and resilient. Far more than I ever gave her credit for before this experience. I'm staring at the woman who fortifies my soul, looking at me for direction, help, confirmation, comfort.

"I'm going to do it."

Absently smudging my nose with the knuckles on my right hand, I walk across to stand behind her to stare at Djinn's words,

"Don't."

"Why not? This won't stop until I give in."

She sounds close to tears; probably holding on with her eyelashes at this point.

"Cindy, please, just give them a chance to help us before you sell your soul to a book."

"I don't like them, I don't trust them. I have a really bad feeling about this."

"But I **do** like them. They know stuff we don't. At least give it twenty-four hours. You were so hesitant before, don't give in to the pressure."

She snaps Djinn closed and stands to face me.

"They have one day, and then we're doing things my way."

SLAM.

The hair on my forearms raises up as much as her eyelids when the door slams behind me. Rushing to it, I yank.

It doesn't budge.

Charging to the sash window, I shove it up.

"Graham!"

The used car salesman doppelganger walks around the corner to look up at me.

"We're locked in!"

Heather comes careening across the lawn to shriek, "It's Abraxis! It's a demon!"

Crap!

"What the fuck am I supposed to do?"

Risking a glance at Cindy, she's a step behind me looking jaundiced. Heather's words are freaking her out.

"Jump!"

I look down at the grass and geranium bushes. Nothing will soften the fall.

Reaching behind me, I move as fast as I can. Before Cin can object or stall, I have her out the window, holding her by an ankle and a wrist.

"Sasha! Oh Jesus," she says staring at me with fear.

"Graham, you'd better catch her or I'll kill you myself."

He nods, and from up here I can see the patch on his crown where he's balding.

Holding my breath, straining muscles I haven't used since mountain climbing, I drop her. Graham gives under the weight, but they're both safe. Standing upright, deciding how to do this, the sash grinds in a screaming slam.

"Fuck."

Djinn

Ribbing fingers through my hair, I look around.

"Let me out!"

Running to the door, I yank on it again. It may as well be epoxied close. Becoming out of breath, I can hear them shouting for me. Pulling out my phone, I redial Heather.

"I can't get out. I'm stuck."

"Burn the book," she says.

"Don't you fucking dare."

Cindy's voice is as clear as if she is holding the phone.

She's willing to sacrifice me over Djinn?

Are you kidding me? Ending the call, I look at Djinn with renewed determination. Her words are enough to solidify the decision. Stomping to it, I heft it up, shunting the third dresser drawer out with my left hand. Dumping Djinn inside it, I pick up the lighter fluid and unpocket the lighter.

"Let me out, or your ass is mine."

The door never creaks, and an unholy squeal from it peels my courage. Whisking around, the door stands open, taunting.

My scalp is rippling, my mouth is too dry to swallow, and I'm on the edge of hyperventilating.

Picking Djinn up again, I walk over objecting floorboards, forcing myself not to run.

"If you pull any weird shit with me, I'll burn you."

Through the threshold, down the steps, through the fringe, almost there ... I yank on the brass doorknob. My hand sticks to it.

It burns like a motherfucker.

Like vengeful dry ice, it's so cold my skin adheres to the metal. Flexing my jaw as I grit teeth in agony, I open the door regardless and stare out at a glorious day through tearing eyes.

"Let go you evil bastard."

It holds on, impossibly colder before turning scalding. A cry of wounded terror opens my throat before I clamp my mouth shut, choking on the pain. Every tendon pops out and my soul shudders with the animalistic yelp that comes from me.

When it repels my hand, I stagger backwards from the force, focusing on raw blisters and blood. Unhesitant, I dive through the door, hurling Djinn backwards over my head into the house like a basketball player with too much talent.

Emotion overwhelms me and I kneel on the paving, doubled over, favoring my hand.

The door shakes the rafters when it flings itself closed. I'm evicted.

A grasp on my shoulder, "Are you okay?"

Shrugging it off, I look up into traitorous blue eyes, "Don't touch me."

Struggling to my feet, I lope to the side of my home to locate the Black's.

Heather spies me first and comes running over like a penguin learning to walk when her shiny heels sink into soft lawn, "Sasha! Thank God."

Her focus darts to my hand, "Graham, medikit. Stat!"

Running her touch over my shoulder and down my back, she guides me to their Prius, "It's okay honey. We know what it is. We'll take care of it from here."

Cindy is giving Heather her death stare again as she joins us. Collapsing into the passenger seat while Graham inspects my hand, I glare right back at her. Challenging.

"How's your hand?" she asks.

"What the fuck do you care?"

She folds her arms and poses with one leg propping her up, "And what's your problem?"

"Cindy, just go home."

"No. Tell me why you're suddenly so eager to get rid of me?"

"You chose a book over my own safety. You can get home from here. I don't think Para-Dice will be requesting your

Djinn

patronage again."

"Jesus Sasha! This bitch wanted to burn it! Do you know how rare a book like that is?"

"Yes, I do. Thanks for your concern."

Turning to face forward, I dismiss her, exchanging a glance with Graham. He gives the briefest of nods, acknowledging silently that the biggest problem is definitely Cindy.

Heather offers, "We can give you a ride home, sweetie."

"I'm not your fucking sweetie," she replies with spiteful vitriol.

We watch in silence as Cindy marches away toward her home. My hope cracks and shatters watching her leave. Her spine is rigid enough to look brittle, her body language tells me I've betrayed her.

Maybe my emotions got the better of me.

"How do you get rid of a demon? How did you know?" I ask Graham.

"Abraxis, he's the demon of genies. Djinn is **the** genie king, which is how I deduced it was Abraxis. If you know anything about Goetia demon worship, you'll know that entire book is a sigil to summon him into our plane." He rests back on his haunches after securing the dressing, an expression of remorse twisting his face, "I'm so sorry, Sasha. We should have thought of it earlier."

Heather joins her husband, perching on the sidewalk, "I knew when it took hold on me. I'm gifted in the paranormal and extracted his identity. He's awful ..." She shudders, looking down, gripping dainty hands with peach fingernails together in her lap, "He has snakes for feet. All hissing and licking and spitting and slithering –" She inhales deeply before meeting my gaze with cloudy green eyes, "And Cindy has a blood bond with him. You can't blame her Sasha. We have to save her before it's too late."

Graham clears his throat, "One other thing. Para-Dice – do

Poppet

you realise your home is named after the Urim dice?"

"The what?"

"They summon spirit messages, and messengers, to the Earth dimension. Your home is a portal, Sasha. If anyone is to blame here, you are."

Djinn

 Chapter 9

Cindy:

He's got the hots for that hillbilly backwards southern wannabe. What is it about short redheads anyway, why do men always find them irresistible? If it's hot he wants, I'll show him redheads have no fire compared to a Cinder.

I refuse to cry because of what he did.

After showering and changing, I drive to church to speak to the comtesse. Huddling inside my pink jumper which matches the streaks in my hair, I rush down the cobbled path to their front door and enter the Sacred Church of La Comtesse de la Nuit. Pierre appears out of the darkness on my right.

"I'm sorry, we're closed."

"Why? I need to speak to the Comtesse."

"She's been ill."

A baritone shouts across the reverent silence, "You are not welcome here. Get out!"

Looking at Jaques, I'm confused, "Why? I've been coming here for years."

"This is your fault! Get out, and don't ever come back."

Pierre takes this as an instruction, gripping me by the upper arm and escorting me forcefully out the door.

"I didn't do anything!"

Jaques' face peeks through the gap where black eyebrows

draw together in an ugly scowl, "You will burn for this. You're evil. Stay away."

The door slams and locks.

I'm speechless. I don't even know what to think.

Dawdling back to the Mini, I'm wondering what to do?

I may as well go to work. I'll just tell them I'm feeling okay now.

Sighing heavily, I start the engine and direct the car into trickling traffic. I'm torn between wanting to hate Sasha with all my heart, and wanting to win him back from that evil cow's claws. She has a husband already, she can't have him too.

Walking through the Collins gallery on my way back to my desk, I stop dead on the colorful carpet under the skylight, staring at the shadow against the wall.

The man turns and looks straight at me.

Every inch of my body turns cold at the soulless eyes. His veins crisscross his scalp like old lace embroidered with purple scars.

Fear runs sharp fingernails between my shoulder blades.

Almost dropping the files, I run to the door, not looking back.

I'll never take that shortcut again.

After telling Nora I am off to see the doc, I charge down stately steps, gripping the polished banister for support as I make my way down to marbleized pillars and high ceilings, before heading to the ground floor, fleeing the spiritual anarchy all around me.

They're everywhere, materializing shadows, latent hauntings, whatever they are, I'm trapped and can't breathe.

I have to get out.

Walking fast through the arches of the main library with its huge windows down both sides, the history of the building suffocates me.

Djinn

Rounding the shelving, I bump into a book trolley, slamming my knee into the blasted thing.

Pitching head first, becoming hysterical, I scramble like a foal off the floor and to the door, birthing into overcast daylight. Sinking onto the steps, my legs too shaky to hold me, I breathe.

And breathe.

Closing my eyes, I hide tears.

Finding the strength to escape, staring down firmly, I avoid feet and shadows, trotting to the car, hiding in it and sobbing.

I can't do this. It's too hard.

Sniffing, wiping my eyes and nose, I phone Rachel.

"I need to see you."

"After work, can we go for a drink?"

"See you then."

Buttressing my courage, I choose to confront Sasha. Engaging first gear, ignoring the strange stares I know I'm receiving, I head into afternoon traffic.

I don't understand how this day started off with so much sunshine and now looks like twilight. It's ominous, like an omen.

I don't get it.

How can someone love me from afar for so long and turn their back on me in a morning? What did she say to him when they were alone in his car? What did she **do** to him? A spell? A hex? Did she curse me?

Who the fuck is she?

She's screwed with the wrong girl. He's mine, and so is Djinn. She can't have either of them.

She thinks she has all the answers, well I know a thing or two myself.

Diverting my path, I go home first. Heading up to the second floor, I rush into my sterile silent home.

A desperation has my jugular, sucking on me like a leech; I have to get him back. Frantic, I open the bottom kitchen drawer

Poppet

and take out the candles, putting them straight into a pot and turning the heat on.

While it melts, I amble to the chair he sat against last night, running my hand carefully over it, dropping to eye level to stare across carpet and then the chair. Finding two sandy hairs, I pick them up, gripping them in tweezered fingers, and deposit them into the wax.

Paraffin candles melt quickly and they're promptly ready. I take the pot off the stove and fill the sink with cold water.

Working quickly, I fashion a poppet to represent him, sealed with his DNA from the hair I found. It's easy when you pour the wax into cold water, it's like working with gum.

Using what's left of the wax, I yank out three of my own hairs and make a poppet to represent me.

They're crude, but intention is everything. This will work, I know it will. Putting them in the ice-box to harden, I go through to the bedroom to get red and black thread, along with my perfume.

Back in the kitchen, I take my poppet out first, spraying it liberally with the fragrance. Withdrawing his, I sit at the kitchen table, inhaling deeply to find my calm place.

Concentrating, I bind us together with the red thread, repeating the mantra. "I bind you together forever. I bind you together forever. I bind you together forever. I bind you together forever ..."

I stop only when I've run out of thread. Satisfied, I take the poppets and put them in the bottom of my closet in my magic box.

Going back to the kitchen with pen and paper, I write her name in bold across the page.

HEATHER BLACK

Rolling it up tightly, I secure the black thread around it. As I start winding, I repeat the next mantra.

"I bind you from doing harm. I bind you from doing harm. I

Djinn

bind you from contact with Sasha Lewis. I bind you from contact with Sasha Lewis. I bind you from doing harm. I bind you from doing harm. I bind you from contact with Sasha Lewis ..."

After three minutes, I snap the thread and move to the lounge. I keep an orange lighter next to the sand bowl, picking it up I set flame to the paper.

Holding it so it burns slowly over the sand, I repeat, "I burn you out of my life. I burn you out of my life ..." until the entire roll is charred black paper.

I stir the burnt shards into the bowl to hide the evidence, purified with the frankincense in the sand.

Lighting the cinnamon incense, I place four burning sticks upright in the sand to mask the smell of wax and burnt paper.

Sitting back, feeling in control again, I light a Marlboro and inhale deeply.

Walking back to the kitchen to run boiling water through the wax pot before placing it into the dishwasher, I then go back to the bedroom and spray my aura cleanser all over myself and the apartment.

Dousing perfume on my hair and clothes to mask any residual burning smells, I make my way out the door, deciding to get a session of reiki to help me relax and fix my chi. Mr Wong is a fabulous little Chinese man I've been going to for over a year.

I know he'll make a plan for me.

It doesn't take longer than fifteen minutes to pull up at his house. Three other cars block his driveway. Unhappy with this, I park out of the way. Walking past the koi pond, I take a moment to watch the fish, immediately calmer just being here.

On entering the Asian home with its bamboo blinds and bonsai trees, the simplicity of the interior brings the first smile I've had all day. Putting my name next on the list, I sit down on

Poppet

the woven floor mat and pour myself a cup of camomile and green tea. The scent of jasmine tea permeates the air and I stare at the two other women meditating on mats and wonder which of them had the jasmine.

Sipping the hot brew, the ambient sounds of healing bowls gonging and ringing gives my overactive imagination relief through hidden speakers. No spooks here, no demons; just tranquility.

I thought bonsai are Japanese. I should ask him about that.

Closing my eyes, I sit in the lotus position after removing my shoes, and begin my meditation.

I have no idea how long I sat like that, but when I open my eyes the other ladies are gone.

"Cindy. How nice suhplise. Come thlough."

I smile at him, he's far too young to be a doctor of anything. But then the Chinese always look young no matter how old they are.

Leaving my shoes at the door, I follow him into the reiki room. It's with relief and a sense of hope that I lay down on the narrow mattress on the massage table. He makes noises with his hands, slapping them together in sweeping motions. Then rubbing his palms together briskly, he stands behind me, holding a hand an inch away on either side of my head.

Breaking habit, he moves to my ankles and repeats the process.

"Some-ing wlong. What you done lately?"

He shakes his head, frowning hard.

"I've had a really bad night."

Holding up a hand, he says, "One minute."

Moving to the light switch, he turns it down low, staring at me a meter away from the table.

"Bad engie. Very bad engie. You have mahk in aula. Like

Djinn

b'and."

Suffocating the tension messing with my heart rate, I ask, "Can you fix it?"

"Sohee Cindy. Nothing can do fo' you. This bad. Vely bad. You need holy week."

Sitting up, I can tell he doesn't want to come anywhere near me. He turns the lights up again, highlighting the neutral tones in his eco-friendly environment.

"Mr Wong, tell me what to do."

"You go mountain, wash in liver, bleathe clean aih, play."

"Meditate?"

He nods vigorously, "Many time. No shoe, you walk on eahth, no shoe. Wash in mountain wahtah. Weep and heal. I no can help."

He ends the session by pulling open the rice paper screen.

"My apology. I no can help."

Getting off the table, I walk past him and through the door, "Thanks Mr Wong."

A brand in my aura? How's that even possible?

And how am I supposed to find the time for a holy week up in a mountain with a river to wash in, cry and pray? Not practical.

I'm disappointed, but his eyes burn a hole through my neck as I collect my shoes and go back outside. Sitting on the edge of the pond, staring through the moon gate while I put my sneakers back on, I'm rejected again when I hear his door lock and the closed sign appear in the window.

I wonder if Sasha will reject me again too?

Why won't anyone help me?

I feel like the ghostly white koi under the calm water. Lost in depths that lead nowhere.

⛥

Chapter 10

Sasha:

Shellshocked, I stare at Graham and Heather.

"What do you mean Urim dice?"

Heather looks to Graham, receives a nod, and starts explaining to me.

"Urim and Thummin are dice used for the revelation of truth. However these dice are also used for evil divination, assigned first to King Solomon who used them in Goetia worship to summon evil to do his bidding. They're a form of communication between realms. Sometimes used for good, as in the revelation of light truth with angelic beings, and sometimes used to summon demons and communicate with them."

She may as well be speaking in tongues, as I haven't a clue what she means.

"What is Goetia?"

"Goetia is a name for sorcery. The oldest in existence. The only kind assigned to the bible and King Solomon."

"Sorcery, how?"

"To summon seventy-two demons. There is also a magical triangle which assigns the relating seventy-two names of God. There's a disturbing cross over in this practice which leads us to believe all divination involving the number seventy-two, relates to wicked intent and communication. King Solomon apparently

Djinn

employed these demons to help him build his temple."

"Who owns them. What for?"

"They are originally traced to the Israelites and their God. They were given to them by God."

"So how can they be evil?"

"That's a long story. Suffice to say, the original intention may have been communication with God, but this practice was corrupted over time as they are so powerful they can summon anything beyond this realm."

"Are you saying that book is a Goetia book?"

"Yes."

"And my home is named after a demon?"

She looks amused, "No, your home is named after the divination dice. But look at them, both the dice on your sign show the number six. Your subconscious summoning is obvious. You drew that book to you."

Guilt stabs me, "And I gave it to Cindy."

Rubbing my knee in a gesture of comfort, she says, "The Urim and Thummin dice have a sordid history. They were originally given to the Israelites out in the tent in the desert. But later in history, their royal kings and priests have been known to use them to summon spirits and demons."

"But I don't own any such thing. How can my home have anything to do with this?"

"Let's get away from here and we'll explain further."

Graham nods, standing.

At their mercy, I move to the back seat, staring at my home with dread.

Sitting opposite the couple in their home, I can't find an appetite even though the home baked macadamia cookies look delectable.

"Sasha, the dice, their original names are Ur and Tamm.

Poppet

Believed to also belong to the Babylonians as urtu and tamitu, which means oracle and command."

Nodding, I interrupt, "But Djinn is an oracle book."

Graham leans forward, "Yes, the two seem connected." He clasps both hands tightly before revealing, "Sasha, the demon Abraxis is also known as Abrasax and Abraxas. In his angelic form, he is in charge of three hundred and sixty-five levels of heaven, and the days of the year. That oracle book is assigned a page for each day of the year. It's his M.O. It's definitely him we're dealing with here."

Heather adds, "They were used to curse. The original Hebrew word for Urim is Arrim, which means to curse."

My core begins quivering and I deposit my teacup on the table, "Are you saying my home is cursed?"

"It depends. You have two dice, which is important. One may represent Thummin, so they could balance each other out. They were used to determine who is innocent and who is guilty."

Heather smirks, "When only two were used, they were used similarly to an Ouija board, essentially giving yes and no answers."

"Like my place? The two dice?"

Graham offers a hollow smile, "Except yours both show the number six. And both are red."

"So?"

"Sasha, you've heard of the Philosopher's stone?"

Looking at Heather, I want to laugh, "I've read Harry Potter."

Except she's not laughing, she looks judge serious.

"It was red, belonging to an angel who will be used to smite, with fire, it's known as carbuncle. The elusive carbuncle stone is also known as the Philosopher's stone."

"The angel Lucifer?" I ask, worry wringing my stomach again.

"No, not him. But this entire issue with your house boils

Djinn

down to intention. You have the magical divination dice depicted on your home, both are red, representing the burning coal – or carbuncle, one that is listed in the top row of the ephod –"

Fuck, this is getting annoying. "What's an ephod?"

Graham answers this time, "The breastplate worn by the Israelite priest, the Levite priest."

"So what's the significance?"

"It's a hierarchy stone because it's in the top row," Heather says.

Leaning back, folding my arms, despairing, I demand, "What the hell does this have to do with my house evicting me?"

"Your sign is lit."

I raise my eyebrows at Graham's cryptic answer.

"The stones in the ephod lit up to answer a question. These rays of light purportedly came from God. Each tribe of Israel was assigned one of these dice, which are magnetic gemstones, and they were employed to communicate beyond our realm into the ethereal plain."

I nod for him to continue.

"Because the dice on your sign are lit, you are constantly broadcasting to the unseen realm."

"And what am I broadcasting?"

"Djinn answers that for you. You're calling demons with that red six. On the ephod the twelve tribes were split into two sections of six. You have two dice with the number six showing, representing splitting up the tribes and their unity. This practice was marked in the New Testament as an instruction which came from the evil god Molech and his henchman Rephan."

Moving my attention to Heather and her answer, I ask the professionals, "So how do we fix this?"

"The stones used for Urim and Thummin are opposite for different tribes of Israel. Which means both stones can be used to summon wicked beings. I think your dice are both the bad ones

81

because both are coloured red," Heather continues. "First you have to take that sign down, disconnect it, and smash it to smithereens. Then change the name of your establishment."

"And then what?" I really want to know when I can go home again.

"Then you get rid of Djinn, and we cleanse your house of residual evil."

Staring at the two of them, "How do we get rid of Djinn? That house wanted to kill us all."

"Throw it into the ocean."

Laughing with derision, I argue, "We'll never get that far."

Graham nods, "We bind it first."

"How?"

"It would be best for you not to know."

"Let's do it," I say.

"It's going to take a little time. Do you have somewhere you can stay tonight?" Heather asks.

I nod, digging out my phone and calling Jerome.

"Jerry, hey dude. Listen, I have an exterminator taking care of a problem at home today. I can't go in until the issue is dealt with. Can I crash at your place tonight?"

"Cool, thanks dude. I'll be at your place this afternoon, in about an hour or so. That cool?"

Nodding, smiling at them to indicate it's a go, I thank him and disconnect.

"Now what?" I ask, looking at them.

"Now you should get hold of Cindy. She needs help."

"But if we bind Djinn and get rid of him, she'll be okay right? She doesn't even have to know."

"That's true. Okay, give us a day and then check on her," Graham says.

Relieved they're not going to pull any exorcist shit on my girl, I'm impatient. "Shouldn't we get cracking?"

Djinn

"We'll take you home to get your car so you can get to your friend's. Let us deal with Djinn and Abraxas. We'll call you when it's done."

Smiling, I stand, offering a hand to Graham, to shake, "Thanks so much for everything."

Two hours later, alone at Jerry's, I use his computer to get a peace offering. I know Cindy is pissed, and I'd better not show up at her door empty handed. I refuse to give her anything from the shop, all the stock is going into one huge bonfire tomorrow, so instead I look for something as unusual as she is.

Grinning, I find a Burlesque place right here in Portland. PDX Pole Divas even offer gift certificates, and I purchase one without hesitation. She's going to love this.

Chapter 11

Cindy:

I've been knocking on his door for six minutes, with no answer. Surrendering to the possibility he's off shagging the redhead from hell, I decide to phone him and ruin his adulterous rendezvous.

"Hello?"

"Hi Sasha, it's Cindy."

Silence greets me.

"Lis ..."

"Sasha, I –"

We speak at the same time. Laughing uncomfortably, I speak into the stilted silence, "I'll go first. I'm outside your door, I came to apologise, but you're probably not home right?"

"No, I'm at a friend's place."

A friend called Heather Black? Is her soul as black as her name?

"Oh ..." I'm not sure what to say.

"Listen Cin, I'm sorry about the way things went down this morning."

"It's okay. I'm sorry too."

Not really, because that cow was going to burn Djinn and you were going to do it for her because you're so desperate to impress her. But I don't want to be alone and I don't want her to have you.

"I'm going out for drinks later with Rachel. Do you wanna

Djinn

come?"

"Yeah, okay. Where're ya gonna go?"

"We're going to Danté's, then I want to go out for Cajun."

"Cool, I'll meet you there. What time?"

"Eight."

"What time are you gonna eat?"

"Around nine."

"Mind if I bring a friend?"

It'd better not be that bitch.

"Sure."

"Cool, see you then."

"I'll meet you in the Limbo Lounge. Bye."

―――

Knowing I'm alone, I try his front door. It's unlocked and opens. Like a dirty guilty thief, I glance around and slip inside, quickly closing the door behind me.

Djinn lies on the floor between me and the store. Instinctively I pick it up and smooth a hand over the cover, blowing imaginary dust off it.

"You poor baby. They've been so mean to you."

Cradling Djinn in my arms, I walk into the shop.

I love the smell in here. It's a heady cocktail of old books, oils, fragrances, magic and history. Wandering between the rows of shelves, I finger oracle books, tarot decks, naddred stones on leather necklaces, essential oils, magical blends, incense, and I stop in front of the selection of semi-precious stones.

Staring into a large crystal ball, I caress it possessively. I've always wanted one of these but they're too pricey for my budget.

Touching large rose quartz blocks, salt lights and mixed gems for rune use, a leather bag intrigues me. It's like the bag Sasha got me to take a rune from.

Reaching behind the big stones, I withdraw the bag and

Poppet

automatically smell it. Closing my eyes, it conjures memories of campfires and roasting flesh. It's oddly comforting.

Looking for a price, I can't find one. Turning it, branded into the leather at the bottom is the word Abrasax. Underneath that are a bunch of weird letters which are probably runes.

It has a nice weight to it. Putting Djinn down on the shelf, I widen the drawstring to look inside. They're so beautiful.

Shiny gemstones engraved as amulets in some ancient language and exotic symbols nestle in the shadowed leather.

Looking for a book to explain them, Djinn flops open, the echoing bang in the complete silence is enough to make me drop the bag.

A stone falls out, sliding across the floor. Kneeling, I fish it out of the dust under the shelves, looking at the brilliant faceted gem ground smooth as a river pebble on the edges. It's so pretty. I stand to look at Djinn.

I know the meanings. I am the book that goes with that bag.

I smile at Djinn. He got cross with those meddling idiots. He knew they'd drive a wedge between myself and Sasha. Rubbing the open page with affection, I speak to my only true friend.

"It's your fault he called those morons."

I was trying to protect you.

"How are we going to fix this? Hmm? It's all a mess now."

Use the stones, say the words.

Withdrawing the red one from my pocket, I thumb it absently, staring at the word which appears on the page, alone.

Ablanathanalba.

"What does it mean?"

It's the name for God. Call on God to help you.

"I don't get it."

Thou art the Father. That's what it means. But to work the magic of the stone, with all sacred words, you must use the naros cycle.

Djinn

"What's that?"

Say it forwards, then backwards, then forwards again.

"Oh my god. It's exactly the same both ways."

In ancient times we wrote right to left, not left to right. Before that we wrote top to bottom on a page. All magical words work no matter which way you write. Say the word, it will protect you.

I trust Djinn. I know none of the others do, but we've reached a mutual understanding. So I follow his instructions.

"Ablanathanalba, ablanathanalba, ablanathanalba."

I pocket the stone as an unbelievable sense of peace brings tears to my eyes again.

Picking it up, I hug him tight, "Thank you."

After a lengthy silence in the gloomy room, I put him back on the shelf still open, picking up the pouch and emptying the stones into my palm. There are eleven of them. Twelve if I count the one in my pocket. Each one a different color with a different symbol engraved on it.

"What are these?"

Amulets for protection and divination.

"Oh."

Looking around, I'm overwhelmed with an odd sense of urgency.

"We should go. And please, no more weird shit. I'm taking you home, I said I'd give Sasha a day, so tomorrow I'll choose you, as you asked. Until then I have to hide you and keep you safe. Okay?"

You are already blessed. The stone will protect you and bring you luck.

"We have to go."

You will get your proof and confirmation that I am changing your life to one of abundance, later today.

Whatever.

Putting the pouch in my pocket, I withdraw fifty dollars from my back jeans pocket and leave it next to the cash register. I won't steal from him and there is no price on the bag.

Grabbing Djinn, closing it, I run through the fringe and back out the door.

Experiencing the high of a bank robber getting away with a heist, I take the corner away from Para-Dice and drive toward home. Never knowing at that moment a Prius entered his road and stopped at the exact location I just left.

Walking into my home, I lock the door and open Djinn.

"Where should I put you so no one will find you?"

Behind the desk in the second bedroom.

Hesitating, I ask him a burning desire.

"What must I do to keep Sasha?"

Choose me and everything you desire will be yours, always.

"Okay."

Closing Djinn, I hide him in the study, taking the pouch and putting it inside my magic box. Then I start getting ready for my hot date.

At seven-thirty I drive over to 350 West Burnside. I love the clean parking area and the black sign above black awning, lit with a row of secretive lights. Danté's is in bold yellow and I walk to the entrance with a sense of homecoming. Their music is always exactly what I need and they serve the most divine drinks.

The sky is beginning to spit and I pull my leather jacket tighter around the red corset.

If it's a corset he wants, it's a corset he'll get.

Thank God their music is decent. This place is always welcoming with its red rustic brick and creamy counters infused with harsh throaty music. It's noisy, atmospheric, and just what I needed to blend in. At last I don't feel like I have 'freak' tattooed on my forehead.

Djinn

Ambling past a black booth around a red table, past wrought iron intimate tables in front of the stage, I spy Rachel and Derrick at the bar next to the fire pit.

Putting my elbows onto the underneath-lit countertop, I ask for tequila before giving Rachel a hug. Sitting next to them, I down my drink and order Tiger's Blood with vodka.

"Wow, you're looking hot enough to descend to the first level of Hell," Rachel says with a smile.

I smile back, knowing even Coco Chanel would approve of this red lipstick. Every aspect is chosen with care to woo Sasha back from that fucking redhead. Skin tight black jeans, black boots with stiletto heels, long enough to stab with, a Satan red corset laced up the front with black gossamer ribbon, and a fitted black leather jacket, all highlighting my white hair. I've changed the pink streaks to red and black respectively. I have the red amulet in my pocket, and enough cash to turn my conquest into a raging alcoholic.

I even stopped on my way over and bought illicit green for him to smoke later.

"What happened? What was the urgency?" she asks.

"Sasha's place got really weird last night –"

Derrick interrupts, putting an arm around Rachel to lean his head closer, "If he messed with you I'll sort him out –"

"It wasn't him. It was all weird supernatural stuff. But he called the Phantom Professionals and almost broke up with me before we'd even gelled properly, thanks to that interfering cow."

Derrick picks up my drink and sniffs it, losing interest in girl talk. "What is this?"

"Tiger's blood and vodka."

"Which is?"

"Fruity watermelon laced with coconut. Don't you just love the rich red color, like blood?"

He shakes his head, eyeing my killer outfit, "You're one

wicked woman, Cin."

For some reason this reminds me of the sign outside that says 'Keep Portland Weird'. I wonder how many people twig that weird means supernatural. I'm simply doing my civic duty.

Grinning at him, pinching my drink back, I say as much, "Doing my civil duty darling, that's all."

"You look like a groupie for the Trailblazers," he teases.

"God! I don't even watch basketball. If Sasha thinks that too, I'm giving men up for good."

Rachel changes the subject, "Have you had dinner?"

"No. Sasha and I were planning on going to the Screen Door for Cajun at nine. Wanna come?"

Derrick nods, "Definitely. They're legend."

We fall silent as I watch Sasha and a dark haired guy making their way across to us. He points at his watch when he reaches me, "Limbo Lounge at eight, remember?"

Turning and leaning my elbows on the bar with my spine against it, the pose highlights cleavage and corset. "Hello stranger."

He's instantly distracted, and I'm smugly thrilled.

"Hi, I'm Jerry," the tall dark haired guy says, pushing his hand at me.

I shake it, "Hi. I'm Cin."

"You sure look like sin."

A collective laugh breaks the awkward tension. I smile cattily at Jerry, "Try the Tiger's blood, it'll put you in the right frame of mind."

They order their drinks and we relocate to a table.

Wending our way between people and furniture, I can feel Sasha's eyes scouring me and my outfit. Stopping, I turn and make him bend down so I can speak in his ear, "Stop scrutinizing me. You're making me uncomfortable."

"But I've always wanted to screwtinize you," he says softly

Djinn

into my ear with a salacious smile.

Shaking my head, smiling back, I let him put his arm around me and lead me to the table claimed by our friends.

Sasha:

While I'm looking at her, her eyes change color, morphing from blue to green. It must be the lighting.

Rachel and Derrick seem nice, Cindy is hot enough to vaporize the Arizona desert, and Jerry has hit it off with them too.

Enjoying the moment, using the opportunity to speak to her privately, I share my news.

"I did some research on that demon. Some sources claim he's a god. His legs are snakes which terminate in scorpions. Which makes me think of all those snake worshipping religions and the ones that state enlightenment comes from the snake." Staring intently into her lusty eyes, I share my epiphany, "Even the snake in the garden of Eden is accused of getting us to eat from the tree of knowledge. So knowledge could easily come from this snake being Abrasax."

Cindy:

Abrasax? I found Abrasax stones in his shop.

Wrapping my arms around his neck and kissing it, I side-step, "Let's talk about it later, I'm hungry."

Lifting me with him as he stands, he tells the others, "It's time to feed my girl. Who's coming?"

Giggling, I whisper on our way from the table, "You are."

Poppet

 Chapter 12

Sasha:

It's only a short drive over the river to get to 2337 E Burnside. Parking on the corner of Northeast 24th Avenue, I escort Cindy from my car. Jerry's driving hers and looks comical in the Mini which neatly halts behind my white Honda.

Settling at one of the wooden picnic tables outside, we peruse our menus. They close at ten and we're running out of time.

Cindy drapes herself against my side and whispers, "Let's have the crispy fried oysters for starters."

She definitely has an agenda tonight. My mouth is twitching while I read her expression, making sure she's not yanking my chain. She seems serious.

I nod, smirking, examining the rest of the menu.

We both order the Backyard Burger with pimento cheese and crispy fried onion rings, then wait while the others place orders. The food here is organic and always delicious. You can tell it's quality food even if it's reasonably priced.

Which reminds me.

Leaning toward her, I ask, "Are you working tomorrow?"

She shakes her head, "No. I tried going in to work today and it freaked me out. I told them I went to the doctor and got booked off for the rest of the week."

"You went to work? After the night we had?"

Djinn

Jerry teases, "Wild night eh? You two are incorrigible."

"Why?" she asks, ignoring Jerry.

"I need to get supplies. Fancy going to Trader Joe's with me?"

"Sure. I love TJ's." She licks her lips, "Mmmm, Thai lime-and-chili cashews."

Covering her thigh with my hand, I give it a squeeze under the table and out of sight of the others, "You really love the hot stuff." Whispering into her ear for intimacy, I say, "I love that you're an organic freak like me."

"Pity I can't afford a car like yours."

Rachel speaks across to her, "Get a lottery ticket."

She nods, "You know, that's really not a bad idea." She looks at me, "Can we get one on the way home?"

She's assuming she's spending the night with me. I knew I liked this chick for a good reason. I've never attempted the removal of a corset before. I know my smile is wide, and Jerry's wearing his, 'you lucky bastard' expression.

"Sure babes. Whatever makes you happy," I answer smugly.

We're interrupted with food arriving at the table. It smells better than thanksgiving, and I look at the other plates with interest. Jerry has Creole jambalaya, Rachel has the pecan trout, and Derrick has the smoked and barbecued beef brisket with bacon potato salad. I laugh at the amount of crispy fried oysters put on the table. Cindy chose a winner with everyone.

She smiles demurely, forking one, "Pity the Blend coffeehouse next door has already closed. They'd be perfect to go to next."

"This is like club hopping, but doing it with food," Rachel says.

The two of them share a glance and smile, which silently communicates great affection and a long friendship.

Poppet

We're finally alone after a long evening of camaraderie and friendship. Derrick and Rachel are so cute you want to be them and hurl at the same time. It's plain they adore Cin, and that it's a mutual fondness. The way Derrick teases her assures me she can take my teasing without getting all PMS on me.

My phone rings again, and again I look at the caller ID. With her head on my shoulder, the spliff we're sharing between her fingers, she pushes my hand away.

"Turn it off. Let tonight be about just us."

"I can't Cin. It might be important."

"Heather Black can wait her turn. Right now is **my** turn."

This is emphasized when she swings herself on top of me while talking, and deftly starts undoing the black bow on the top of her corset.

Switching my phone off, I toss it to the other side of the bed, capturing her hands where she sits on my hips, "Hey, I get to do that, not you."

Giggling, she hands me the spliff, "She's called you thirteen times. That's an unlucky number."

Taking a pull and putting it out in the ashtray on her bed, I debate, "Yeah, and you've distracted me from answering every time. If I'd answered, we wouldn't be disturbed now."

"That's what you think. If you'd answered I wouldn't be getting laid tonight, and neither would you."

"That Tiger's blood is some potent shit."

She laughs, "That's because yours was seventy percent proof with codka."

"You mean vodka."

"Yeahm that stuff."

I notice her eyes aren't fully focused on me. She is toasted, and horny.

There is a God. Slowly unlacing the most impractical piece of female clothing I've encountered, I mention the thing in the back

Djinn

of my mind, taunting, "It's been surprisingly quiet tonight."

"Do you know this thing unclips?"

"It does?"

"Yeah, at the back."

Swiveling backwards cowgirl style, I look at the row of hook things.

"That's cool. Pity your jeans are still on or this could be quite the sight."

She waits for it to be undone before turning to face me again, "Before this night is through, you'll have plenty of new material for your poetry scribblings."

"I have a letter for you."

"You do?" her smile makes me feel guilty for the joke.

"A French letter."

"Gah!" she slaps my arm.

"Seriously though, I got you a gift."

She lays on top of me, tracing my chest with a black fingernail, "What is it?"

"Look in my pocket."

"Nah uh. Not falling for more of your dirty tricks."

Chuckling, I move toward her to get my hand in the pocket, presenting her with the gift certificate.

She holds it in trembling fingers, the paper jitters.

Worried, I move to look into her eyes, truly concerned I've fucked up properly when I see she's crying. "What? What did I do?"

Unexpectedly she grabs my head and starts kissing me. "I love it. It's the best present ever."

"Then, why are you crying?"

"Because you're so thoughtful, I don't deserve you."

Cashing in the bonus points, I settle in for more than a kiss after she places it next to her lottery ticket.

Poppet

Sasha:

Enjoying a postprandial smoke, I watch her walk carefully back in wearing her kimono while holding mugs.

"I laced them with Kahlúa."

"You're a closet alcoholic aren't you?" I tease her.

"Yup. I'm a member of the AA. Arcane Addicts."

"Then I'm a member too." Taking the mug, I hand her the smoke and have a sip.

"Actually, did you know it's Mexican? It means *House of the Acolhua people*. They're related to the Aztecs. You're drinking history baby."

"Are you sure you weren't born in a Mayan temple? There's a definite pattern to your food choices."

"I wish I was. Then maybe my life would make sense to me." She pauses between sips, "Makes you think doesn't it? We're drinking a potion created by a civilization who sacrificed people to their gods."

"That's a disturbing thought."

Sipping in companionable silence, she catches my attention when she puts her mug down on the bedside table with a feverish rattle.

"What is it?"

"Can't you see it?"

"See what?"

"This happened to me earlier. I saw ghosts and weird shifting shadows at work. Except the ghost in the gallery looked worse than you expect a ghoul to look."

"What are you talking about?"

Putting my own coffee down, I stare into the shadows beyond the candle arcs.

"Standing there between the closet and the door. Blocking our

Djinn

exit."

Rigid with tension, I stare at the shadows, looking for form or shape, or movement.

Twisting to look at her, her eyes are definitely green again, "I don't see it."

She hides behind me, gripping arms tightly around my chest, "It's coming."

Poppet

 Chapter 13

Cindy:

Dropping Sasha at his house to collect his car, we make our way home to get supplies, stopping first at church to replenish our stock of holy water.

"Father John."

Graham shakes his hand, and I'm finally feeling peaceful and safe. That house was saturated in evil. I shake Father's warm papery hand and shoot Graham a beseeching glance. He acknowledges it.

"Father, we have a problem. Abraxas is loose in Portland. We encountered him this morning."

Sitting together on pews next to royal-red carpeting, we're alone in the church and speak freely.

He nods at Graham, "Go on."

"We know the Archbishop of Calcutta performed an exorcism on Saint Mother Theresa. We'd like permission to use the same rite."

"Graham, the Essenes were the first in our church who used exorcism, and to do it right I must ask you if you've consumed yeast recently?"

"No beer and no bread, Father."

"Good. The sacraments are sacred mysteries which cannot be performed for folly. How do you know you're dealing with

Djinn

Abraxas?"

Taking a deep breath, I start reciting the events. I know he's going to tell us we're unqualified, but we have to try. We don't have the time to wait for papal approval.

Heather:

We look at each other and begin chanting the words of the Third Secret. Kneeling before Sasha's front door, we murmur softly.

"Most glorious Prince of the Heavenly Armies, Saint Michael the Archangel, defend us in our battle against principalities and powers, against the rulers of this world of darkness, against the spirits of wickedness in the high places. Come to the assistance of men whom God has created to their image and likeness and whom Jesus has redeemed at a great price from the tyranny of the devil. Holy Church venerates thee as her guardian and protector; to thee, the Lord has entrusted the souls of the redeemed to be led into heaven. Pray therefore that the God of Peace allows men of faith to expel Satan, that he may no longer retain men captive and do injury to the Church. Offer our prayers to the Most High, that without delay they may draw His mercy down upon us; take hold of 'the dragon, the old serpent, which is the devil and Satan,' bind him and cast him into the bottomless pit, so that he may no longer seduce the nations."

We light the censor together, encircling ourselves with holy smoke.

"In the Name of Jesus Christ, our Lord, strengthened by the intercession of the Immaculate Virgin Mary, Mother of our Savior, of Blessed Michael the Archangel, of the Blessed Apostles Peter and Paul and all the Saints, we confidently undertake to repulse the attacks and deceits of the devil," we say together.

Continuing with the censor, we walk around the house,

purifying it with the temple smoke, "God arises; His enemies are scattered and those who hate Him flee before Him. As smoke is driven away, so are they driven; as wax melts before the fire, so the wicked perish at the presence of God."

I hold up the sanctified cross, "Behold the Cross of the Lord, flee bands of enemies."

Graham says, "He has conquered, the Lion of the tribe of Judah, the offspring of David."

"May thy mercy, Lord, descend upon us," I say.

"As great as our hope in Thee," he says.

Walking back to the front door, we make the sign of the cross on each other, and together on the door with holy water.

"We drive you from us, whoever you may be, and Abraxas, unclean spirits, all satanic powers, all infernal invaders, all wicked legions, assemblies and sects," we make the sign of the cross again. "In the name of the Father and by the power of our Lord Jesus Christ, may you be snatched away and driven from here and from the souls made to the image and likeness of God and redeemed by the Precious Blood of the Divine Lamb."

Looking up, the sky has turned so dark the windows now look like black mirrors. Thunder rolls and peals with the wind roaring up around us, swishing the trees, bringing a cold chill with it.

"He hears us," I say to Graham. Shivers striate my skin and my skirt blows.

"Ignore his petty parlor tricks. Concentrate."

Nodding, we continue, "Most cunning serpent, you shall no more dare to deceive the human race, persecute the Church, torment God's elect and sift them as wheat. The Most High God commands you, They with whom, in your great insolence, you still claim to be equal; Yahweh commands you. The eternal Son commands you. The eternal Holy Ghost commands you. Jesus, God's Word made flesh, commands you; He who to save our race

Djinn

outdone through your envy, humbled Himself, becoming obedient even unto death; He who built His Church on the firm rock and declared that the gates of hell shall not prevail against Her commands you, because He will dwell with Her all days even to the end of the world. The sacred Sign of the Cross commands you," we pause and make the sign of the cross thrice on the door again. "As does also the power of the mysteries of the Christian Faith. The glorious Mother of Jesus, the Virgin Mary, commands you; She who by her humility and from the first moment of her Immaculate Conception, crushed your proud head. The faith of the Holy Apostles Peter and Paul and of the other Apostles command you. The blood of the Martyrs and the pious intercession of all the Saints command you."

Graham stands and kicks the front door wide open. He's such a brutal strong man in the face of evil, he makes me think naughty thoughts.

With his shirt billowing around him, his hair flaying like arms reaching for a rescue, he yells into the hollow chasm of the house, "Thus, cursed dragon, and you, diabolical legions, we adjure you by the living God, by the true God, by the Holy God, by Yahweh 'who so loved the world that He gave up His only Son, that every soul believing in Him might not perish but have life everlasting;' stop deceiving human creatures and pouring out to them the poison of eternal damnation; stop harming the Church and hindering her liberty. **Begone, Satan**, inventor and master of all deceit, enemy of man's salvation. Give place to Christ in whom you have found none of your works; give place to the One, Holy, Catholic and Apostolic Church acquired by Christ at the price of His Blood. Stoop beneath the all-powerful Hand of God; tremble and flee when we invoke the Holy and Terrible Name of Jesus, this Name to which the Virtues, Powers and Dominations of heaven are humbly submissive, this Name which causes hell to tremble, this Name which the Cherubim and Seraphim praise unceasingly repeating: Holy, Holy, Holy is the Lord, the God of Armies."

I whisper, afraid, "O Lord, hear my prayer."

"And let my cry come unto Thee!" Graham bellows.

"May the Lord be with you."

"And also with you," he says to me, resting his palm on my head.

Kneeling back on the porch with me, he holds my hands, "Let us pray. - God of heaven, God of earth, God of Angels, God of Archangels, God of Patriarchs, God of Prophets, God of Apostles, God of Martyrs, God of Confessors, God of Virgins, God who has power to give life after death and rest after work, because there is no other God than Thee and there can be no other, for Thou art the Creator of all things, visible and invisible, of whose reign there shall be no end, we humbly prostrate ourselves before Thy glorious Majesty and we beseech Thee to deliver us by Thy power from all the tyranny of the infernal spirits, from their snares, their lies and their furious wickedness; deign, O Lord, to grant us Thy powerful protection and to keep us safe and sound. We beseech Thee through Jesus Christ Our Lord. Amen."

"From the snares of the devil, deliver us, O Lord."

"That Thy Church may serve Thee in peace and liberty, we beseech Thee to hear us. That Thou may crush down all enemies of Thy Church, we beseech Thee to hear us."

Nodding, we stand, picking up our rosaries, holy water, bibles, and holy ash.

Together we step over the threshold while ozone scorches the air around us and lightning back lights our dramatic entrance.

Tibetan brass healing bowls in the shop all begin their creepy ringing. Wind chimes clash crystal against glass, bamboo wind pipes whistle, cymbals smash, Indian rain sticks shake and rattle, and a god awful stench assaults our nostrils.

"I am not afraid of you, Abraxas!"

Djinn

I trail Graham on his warpath up the stairs. The ceiling pounds, the stairs sound like an army are rushing over the steps in metal boots around us, while the lights flick on and off, competing with the pyrotechnics display in the sky outside. We shouldn't have waited for it to be dark.

He grabs my hand, hauling me with him in aggressive strides to the first floor, their bedroom, and Djinn.

"Say it with me, keep throwing the water, do not fail me Heather."

I nod, "I love you."

"I love you too."

He smiles gently, but his eyes are fierce and distracted.

Turning, we stalk to the bedroom threshold. It slams in my face, blowing the hair off my brow.

He starts yelling, and I add my choral voice, "**Deus, in nómine tuo salvum me fac,**

et virtúte tua age causam meam!"

Splattering holy water at the closed door, I hold my Bible tight over my breast for protection.

Graham smashes his fist wrapped in a rosary into the door, knocking like a man determined to get to his child in the clutches of a pedophile, with amplified angry booms.

"**Deus, audi oratiónem meam; áuribus pércipe verba oris mei!**"

The door falls off the hinges, submitting to him, crashing in a loud bang when it connects with the wooden floorboards.

We take a step toward the room, it flicks back up, tilting and aiming for Graham. I screech my prayer, close to hysterics when it connects him in the chest and he goes tumbling down the stairs.

"**Nam supérbi insurréxunt contra me, et violénti quasiérunt vitam meam; non proposuérunt Deum ante óculos suos!**"

"Graham!"

Poppet

Silence greets me. After the demonic cacophony of noise the immediate silence runs long incisors of fear through my spirit.

I know that fucking book is in here.

Marching in, simultaneously powdering the floor with ash and throwing water at the air in front of me, the lights begin their strobe again, and I can't see Djinn.

"**Ecce, Deus ádjuvat me, óminus susténtat vitam meam!**"

Stomping to drawers, looking under the bed, throwing off the duvet, checking the closet, shrieking over renewed cracks of lightning, "**Retórque malum in adversários meos, et pro fidelitáte tua déstrue ilos! Voluntárie sacrificábo tibi, celebrábo nomen tuum, Dómine, quia bonum est!**"

The duvet lifts and accelerates toward me. Turning, I run out the bedroom, down the stairs, and to Graham. Standing over him protectively, holding up my crucifix and bible, I yell like my life depends on it, "**Nam ex omni tribulatióne eripuit me, et inimícos meos confúsos vidit óculos meus!**"

The bedding floats like a spectre, covering both of us in an instant black shroud. Dropping my weapons, I wrestle to get it off.

"Graham! Say it with me! **Glória Patri!**"

Getting breathing room, I yank where my hand snags the edge, Graham's voice was so weak, I need to see him.

"Graham, talk to me!"

He's not answering.

The floor is shuddering with satanic earthquakes, the doors slam repeatedly, the lights stay off now, but every single thing that can make a noise begins disharmonious discord.

The crescendo raises in pitch, and I fling the duvet out the front door, dragging Graham's heavy body toward the exit, "I know the walls of Jericho, you prick! Noise doesn't scare me! God is here! Run you evil bastard! Go back to hell!"

Becoming breathless with effort, I keep hauling Graham even though my heels refuse traction on the floor. Kicking my shoes

Djinn

off, I pull, "We're nearly there baby. Hang on."

"Satan, I rebuke you! I'm turning the other cheek!" I yell into the dark.

Liquid runs over the floor toward us. That evil demon must have turned on every faucet in the house.

Then he'll probably drop a light on it and watch us cook like burnt sacrifices.

Desperate, at the threshold, I reach to pull on his shirt when he's rudely ripped from my grasp and the door slams in my face.

"**Abaxas**! Abraxas let me in! I rebuke you! You do not belong here!"

My cries are left unanswered, the door remains locked and barred to me.

Trembling violently, hail begins pelting down, battering and breaking with unholy force. Banging on the door, I can't hear it over the noise of the weather.

I don't have any of my tools, this is Sasha's house, maybe it'll grant him entrance. The front door thumps and shakes and I'm terrified Graham's being nailed to the door on the inside. The unmistakable sound of glass panes shattering reaches me.

Graham! Oh my God.

Crying uncontrollably, I manage to find the number and press dial.

"Jesus, help us! Save him!"

Poppet

 Chapter 14

Sasha:

I knew the peace was too good to last.
    She shakes my shoulder roughly.
    "Oh God," she says in a contrite voice.
    Turning, I follow the pointed finger to where the curtains are burning.
    "There's no smoke, it's an illusion," I logically argue.
    In response, the flames quadruple, gobbling up the drapes and licking wildly across to the bed. Snatching my jeans from the inferno, I start shoving legs into denim, "Get dressed."
    "Call 911."
    "Not until I know this is real."
    Standing, buttoning my jeans, I approach the flames. The heat is searing, the carpet melting and too hot to stand on. "And put your shoes on."
    She shakes her head, jumping off the bed to the door and running down the passage into darkness.
    Shit.
    "Cindy!"
    Snatching my phone off the bed, I follow her. The second bedroom light is on. My stomach bottoms out when I look at her with Djinn open on the floor in front of her knees.
    "Sasha, I have to do this. We need the help."

Djinn

"But it's a demon."

"No, it's not. You said your research uncovered it was the first name for God. God's in this book, and it's time He made me a believer. There's no harm in choosing God, is there?"

I can't argue with her there. Now I'm sorry I told her about the research I did on Abrasax and Abraxas.

I incline my head with dissatisfaction, "You have to follow your heart. I'm following mine."

A brief smile changes her severe expression before she returns her focus to the fatigued pages under her fingers. The strangest sensation filters through me, like slipping into warm water.

"Okay. I choose to help you. Now you help me," she tells the book.

It glows like an infrared hand scan around her fingers. The wording changes.

It is done.

Staring at them, I can't help wondering what it is that is done.

Which reminds me, I need to phone Heather. Switching my phone on, I step back into the passage and look down at her room. There is no evidence it was ever on fire.

Turning back while the phone rings in my ear, I ponder aloud, "What was in that green? Are you sure we weren't just hallucinating together?"

"I have no idea. I've never bought it before."

"Sasha!" screams in my ear.

Holding a finger up to Cindy and pointing at the phone, I say, "Heather. Sorry for the delay, my phone was off."

"You have to get home. The police want to speak to you."

My strength drains. Am I being arrested? What did they find in my house?

"Why?"

"There's been an accident."

Poppet

Her sob makes me dread the worst and she disconnects without elaborating.

"We have to go. Heather's crying, the cops want to see me, and apparently there was an accident at my place," I inform Cin, grabbing her hand and rushing us back to the strangely unaffected bedroom and our clothes.

An ear splitting sound like a tree trunk being struck by lightning and every air pocket exploding simultaneously snaps the calm.

With raw nerves and harnessed terror, we walk to the lounge. The Ouija board lies in pieces across the room.

We stare at each other with shocked expressions, neither of us knowing what this symbolizes, or what to say.

Getting out the car, I see Heather standing on my porch, her hair saturated flat around her skull like a crocheted mob cap. A face as pale as yoghurt flashes our way streaked with black tears, giving her a vampiric appearance.

Exchanging a grim look with Cindy, I hold her hand and make my way to the front door pulsating with police, a fire engine and an ambulance's emergency lights.

Stepping onto the porch, Heather silences the officer, turning and laying hands on me, juddering like a spiritual Quaker overtaken with a vision.

"Sasha, this is Officer Davies. I'm so sorry ..."

She bursts into tears and walks away, leaving us confounded and feeling guilty, even though I've no idea what we've done.

"Sasha Lewis," I tell the cop, gesturing to Cindy, "And Cindy Wolfe."

The intimidating muscle-head nods, and gestures to the door, "A word, inside, if you don't mind."

I nod, walking in before him and feeling cornered. Meandering to the lounge, I sit on the couch, still holding Cindy's

Djinn

hand which I'm gripping like a sanity rope.

"Mister Lewis, where were you tonight between eight and twelve?"

Scratching behind my ear, I focus on preventing my voice from wavering, hoping our pupils aren't still dilated, "I met Cindy at Danté's at eight. We were with friends, so we have plenty of witnesses. We left Danté's at about nine, from there we went to the Screen Door for dinner. We stayed until they closed. We all then went back to Danté's. Cindy and myself left there at about eleven. We went back to her place. I'm sure the neighbors could corroborate that."

Cindy's fingers twitch laced between mine, "Why? What did we do?"

"Graham Black was brutally murdered in your home some time between nine-thirty and midnight. Mrs Black was hysterical and her timeline isn't definitive. I believe you gave them permission to be here?"

I exchange a worried look at the news with Cindy before answering. "Yes."

"Sir, may I ask what the nature of their visit to your home was?"

"They were going to cleanse it of negative energy. They're the Phantom Professionals."

The man looks bemused, as if telling us this is hard for him, "Mister Lewis, Mrs Black made a number of outrageous claims. Saying that doors unhinged themselves and pushed her husband down the stairs, that panes broke and he was thrust through them; earthquakes, noises, bangs, water all over the floor, yet as you can see, your home is perfectly orderly."

I look around. I believe Heather but know it would sound nuts to say as much. Instead I mumble, "Yes, I can see that."

"The storm was really bad though," Cindy says, as if in explanation.

Poppet

"How long have you known the Black's?"

I look back at the officer, "Only since yesterday, when I called them."

"So you have no idea if they have a history of mental illness?"

"No sir. I have no clue."

"Mrs Black kept mentioning a demon. Do you know anything about this demon?"

Sighing, I give Cindy's hand a tight squeeze to keep her quiet, "Only what the Black's themselves told me. They said a book I brought into the shop and gave to Cindy here, was possessed with a demon named Abraxas. They came here today to bind the demon and exorcise the house."

"And you believed them?"

I offer a shrug, "They're the professionals, not me."

"Mister Lewis, why did you call them? What was the nature of the problem in your home?"

"A bulb popped and the door blew closed. It got a bit creepy."

"But those are explained logically, are they not?"

"They can be, yes. I just wanted to be certain. Better safe than sorry." I give him an embarrassed grin, milking my moment, implying innocence and ignorance.

He nods, flipping his notebook closed, "Thank you for your time. Sorry about the disturbance to your neighborhood. We thought it was a major emergency."

Cindy asks, "What happened?"

He stands, adjusting his belt, "I'm not at liberty to disclose information in an ongoing investigation."

I add my dissent, "But this happened in my home. We have a right to know."

"Mr Black died today. Mrs Black is the only witness. They were alone here." He gives me a meaningful look as if to say, draw your own conclusions at that boy.

Djinn

Cindy gasps, "Oh my God! How? What happened?"

That's a delayed reaction. He already told us Graham was brutally murdered. I give her another worried glare.

He arcs his neck like he's adjusting it for tension, "I'm not at liberty to say, ma'am."

He nods my way and exits the lounge.

Collapsing into the sofa, I exhale slowly, "Jesus. I thought I was in shit for something."

Cindy sits forward, swiveling and facing the wrong way on the couch, "Do you think she killed him?"

"I doubt it. They seemed like the perfect couple when I was alone with them earlier."

"She's got the hots for you. A woman can tell. Watch, she'll never stop phoning you now. You made her wish she was single."

"Cindy! How can you say that? The woman just lost her husband."

"She killed him."

"I don't know about that. She had no motive to kill him, and after the things we've seen lately, I wouldn't be surprised if something supernatural did go down in here today."

"Let's go ask her," she says, getting off the couch and pulling on my hand.

Walking quickly back outside, I'm led like a naughty dog being taken out, only to see Heather handcuffed and being escorted into the back of a police car. Our eyes connect and shame and guilt itch my insides again.

"How do we defend her without sounding crazy? Plus I'll never pass a drug test."

Cindy turns and wraps slender arms around my waist, staring up at me with soulful eyes, "You don't. We've lost too much in this life already. We can't afford to lose each other too, or our homes, just because the expert exterminators took on a job they couldn't handle."

Poppet

Staring down, I want to believe her, but I feel like such a shit.

Djinn

 Chapter 15

Sasha:

What does the body look like? Is what they're accusing her of even possible? She's a diminutive woman who walks around in high heels. Graham was still strong and in no way do I believe Heather could overpower him in a confrontation.

"I want to see the body," I tell Cindy.

Unravelling her arms, I walk alone to the ambulance, "Excuse me, where will I find Mr Black's body?"

The medic points to the black body bag.

"Why are you still here?"

"Waiting for the chief, then we're taking this guy to the morgue."

"What about an autopsy?"

How can they not perform an autopsy in a murder investigation?

"We'll see what the chief says."

Looking at the disinterested man, I ask, "Mind if I take a look?"

"Help yourself, just don't touch him or you'll screw up any DNA evidence."

I nod, "I won't, thanks."

Before someone sees me and prevents me from taking a look, I climb into the back and unzip the top half of the bag. Fear has

Poppet

my throat so tight my eyes are watering.

The skin on his chest is in tatters, knitting with the cotton of his torn shirt; my gaze soaks in the details like a tissue dropped on blood. The smell is overwhelming. He reeks of being passed through the intestines of Leviathan and pooped out the other side.

Drinks and dinner lurch halfway up my gullet before I clamp my muscles and hold my breath. His eyes are wide like magic 8 balls because his eyelids are missing, glazed and milky, netted with burst blood vessels.

I can hear footsteps clomping closer, but can't look away from the mark; the fresh blistered pink brand on his neck.

What is that? Glass? The stuff is embedded all round his neck like he walked through a tornado of crystal instead of hail.

Following the congealed blood trail, I unzip further to look at his hands. They're skinned and swollen. He put up a fight against something hard, definitely.

Maybe Heather locked him in and he was trying to get out?

There's bruising around both eyes and a deep slash in his hair to his forehead.

Wait.

Peering intently at it, I know a sigil when I see one. It's mostly hidden by his hair.

What the fuck were they doing in my house? Blessing it or cursing it? How do I know they're not part of some freaky cult invoking evil, instead of expelling it? There are too many cuts, like a rite happened. These are slices with pattern and intent.

This feels all wrong.

Repulsed, I drop the plastic coffin and zip it back up.

Everything I believed about them has just disintegrated.

Could she have done it? We're capable of doing anything when pushed hard enough.

Or possessed.

"Sorry sir, you're going to have to leave, we've got our

Djinn

orders."

Nodding, backing away, still unable to divert my eyes from the lump that was Graham, I slip and fall out the back when the guy grabs my arm and catches me from smacking my head on the tread plate.

I'm disoriented, like I'm severely slammed on drugs and booze. Sitting heavily on the grass, the white headed witch comes to sit in front of me, rubbing my arms.

"Are you okay?"

Pushing the hair off my forehead, I lean into my hand and stare down at the space between us.

It's cold.

I'm like an abscess about to burst. Something's building, welling up inside me. Violently shoving her back, I throw up on the grass.

I can handle my shit. This isn't overindulgence, it's a gut reaction to something intensely evil. Bile burns my throat, hacking and regurgitating until there's only spittle and a soul deep sour fear, I cough.

That's my home. Defiled.

I don't think I can ever go in there again. If Para-Dice summons and manifests demons, they had their sacrifice tonight.

We sit out there together until we're all that's left of the mayhem.

"Shouldn't we go inside?"

I shake my head.

"Sasha, what is it? Tell me what happened?"

Adding insult to injury it starts raining azure confetti on us. I have a desperation I can't explain. A hopelessness.

"Okay, now you are freaking me out. Are you in shock? Do you need a drink, or a smoke, or summin?"

Poppet

"He was a stench bucket. He smelled **really** bad."

"Come on, let's get you inside, you're shivering."

"He had no eyelids. Like a fucking zombie just staring and stinking."

"Honey, it's raining, come on, help me get you up."

"With a brand on his neck."

Cindy flops back down, giving me her sinner at confession stare, "He what?"

I'm shaking. How long have I been shaking like I have DT's?

Maybe it is shock.

It's bloody freezing out here.

"I don't want to go back in there, we'll go back to your place." I give her a debilitated smile, "You can work your mojo on me again and make me all better."

"Wait, Sasha –"

But I'm walking. I can't get away from here fast enough. I'm fleeing like I was the murderer at this crime scene, in the Honda, and reversing back to pick her up before I'm properly aware. I can't drive like this. What the hell, man?

"The house is still open –" she says as she opens the door.

"I don't care! Just get in damn it!"

When the door slams shut, I don't even get annoyed. Usually that would piss me off, but it's taking all my focus to follow the blurring street lights back to her place. I'm badly zonked. Tripping out on fear.

How we got there I'll never know, the next moment I'm in her lounge and she's caressing my forehead.

"You're burning up baby."

"Yeah, I'm not feeling too hot."

"You're going to combust if you get any hotter. And I don't mean that in a sexy way."

Shutting my eyes I collapse back, inhaling, the world rotates in opposition to my orientation, making me nauseous.

Djinn

I jolt, snapping them back open when she touches me, smacking and blocking out of reflex. I didn't even hear her move away.

"Sasha!"

Crap. I just knocked half a glass of water over the table.

"Just drink these and go and lie down. I'm not very good with the nurturing thing and you are really freaking me right now." She shoves what's left of the water at me, offering tablets in her other hand, water trickles down her collarbone, capturing my attention.

Sitting up, I take the pills, swallow, relax.

Cold. So frost cold.

I need a shower.

Shoving myself upright, I stagger in the direction of the bathroom.

Sandpaper. Who the hell is sandpapering at this hour? My eyelids seem glued together. Rolling onto my back, I force them to open, unsticking, they're raw and painful, like I've been crying, or caught in a smoke-bomb raid.

Delia once sprayed me with her mace, that's what this feels like.

That noise is fraying my patience fast.

Sitting up, I reach for the light.

Wait.

Hang on.

I must be at Cindy's? Where's the light?

Is it really that hard to have a light on both sides of a bed? Plan ahead goddam it.

Flipping back the duvet, I stomp to the wall and feel for the switch. Turning it on, it occurs to me that the sound's now coming from behind me. Twisting so fast I yank my hamstring, I face the

Poppet

room.

Instantly weak, my legs turn into straws of goop, and I sag into the wall to keep standing.

Oh Jesus!

That's a hobo spider.

Every blood corpuscle I have is trying to burrow inward with terror, rendering my extremities useless.

I don't have the courage.

Backing out of the room, slowly, fixated on the funnel spider sitting halfway into her mouth with its fat patterned abdomen, I gape at its long legs rest carelessly over her lip to her chin.

I hate being male. Why the fuck do we always have to rescue women from spiders?

I can't.

Out the room, I turn and leap into the bathroom like I'm fire walking on hot coals, closing and locking the door behind me.

God.

Sweat runs down my arm to my elbow, pooling on my knee when I rest on my legs, sitting on the closed loo, staring desperately at the floor.

Now what do I do?

Djinn

Chapter 16

Sasha:

Tired of hiding and desperately needing sleep, I creep carefully around the place to the kitchen. With a pot lid for squashing and a duster for flicking, ever watchful for more covert attackers with more than two legs, I steel myself for the confrontation of my life.

Inside the doorway, using the lid like a gladiator shield, I shimmy, dancing karate spar style toward her, and the pet spider causing her to snore like a wood boring beetle.

Gaaah, I can't get bugs out of my head.

Shuddering involuntarily, I stab at the thing with the feathered end, it raises two legs up and looks ready to pounce.

"Fuuuuhck."

Hopping back behind the door, gulping breaths, I'm a six-foot-three mass of tremors. Retreating to the lounge, I pace, wondering what to do.

This is bullshit. I won't be defeated by an arachnid.

Striding back to the bedroom, ready for confrontation number two, I dive out from my cover of the door, wary as a priest at a séance.

Look at that smug prick. You're going to die you piece of shit.

Batting for a home run, I connect feathers with Cindy's face.

The spider is flung directly onto the drapes and Cindy adds to the dramatics by pegging upright and screaming like I just stuck a voodoo needle in her eye.

Sympathetically screaming myself because I'm so strung out, I lunge at the monster with a battle cry, clanging pot lid into wall and drape simultaneously.

Smashing it down repeatedly, tension has me rigid, even my neck feels like it's in a brace. I only lift the lid when I see a leg broken off and sticking macabre-like to the material.

"What the hell!"

"Spider!" I grunt back in explanation.

She screams again, which has my nerves reacting like a marionette having all strings pulled at once.

Leaping backwards, well out of spider jumping range, I stare at the squishy mess on the curtain. Relieved, I flick a panicked look her way.

"Go wash your face. That bastard was in your mouth."

Her hand raises automatically to her lips and she convulses like she's going to throw up. Diving out of bed, she runs for the bathroom.

Sitting down, nervously smoothing an eyebrow with my thumb, I wait for her to return, feeling queasy myself.

When she returns, her face is pink from scrubbing.

"I get the impression dating you will never be dull."

She stares at the mess on her cream curtain, "Maybe it's you that's made this crazy."

"That flipped me out, Cin."

"How did you even know? What made you wake up and look at me? Or are you just a creep who gets off watching people sleep?"

"You couldn't breathe and it sounded like someone was sandpapering with the way you were snoring. That's what woke me." Giving her my 'you suck' glare, I say, "I don't do weird

Djinn

creepy stuff. Thanks for the accusation."

"You know Sasha, I'm finding dating you just as stressful. No sleep, walking furniture, hiding in cemeteries, being questioned by cops, murder, demons, and talking books, none of this is conducive to getting laid. None of it."

"What time is it?"

"What's that got to do with anything?"

"Cinderella, what is the fucking time?"

"Six."

"Let's go for breakfast, then let's escape. Let's just run away for three days."

"Where're we gonna go?"

"The Shaman."

"Who's the shaman?"

"A friend of mine. You, me, naked in a sweat lodge, now we're talking."

"Okay, I'm sold, but you have no clothes."

"Nope, we'll grab some after getting supplies to take with us from Trader Joe's. We can only take biodegradable supplies, so TJ's is the place to go. I'll get some new jeans and stuff on our way out to Breitenbush."

"Is that where he lives?"

"Right on the river, it's gorgeous and just what we need."

"Can we also go to Two Dragon Herbarium?"

"What for?"

"They have some awesome teas and supplies that would fit the whole spiritual journey thing. And I'm thinking some of their pheromone products might be fun to try."

"Like you need more pheromones in your arsenal."

"Okay, you get the shower first, I'll make coffee, then we swap, and go grab brekkers."

I pat her leg, pleased. Feeling possessive, the thought of shagging her in a sweat lodge is pretty much all I can think of right now.

Walking to the shower, I can't wait to wash spider remnants off me. Thank God she doesn't panic like other women do. She's tougher than she looks.

Cindy:

"Tell me again why we couldn't just go to your place to get your clothes?"

"I can't go in there yet. I just can't."

Turning my attention back to shelves of glass jars filled with herbs, I focus on getting my supplies. I end up selecting a bag of eucalyptus leaf, and frankincense gum powder for the sweat lodge. I can't resist fajita seasoning, orris root, vanilla beans, turmeric powder and Cajun spice powder for my kitchen.

Watching him staring at the tea supplies, I hide a smile as I get ginseng root powder and guarana seeds, to add to our drinks at the Shaman's, in case we need the stamina.

Oh look, sweet violet leaf to dry up colds and mucous. I'm definitely getting that because I'm beginning to get a bit heady like I have a bug coming on.

Circling back to see what he's selected, it's probably a good idea that, Blood Cleanser tea. Makes sense for a spiritual cleansing to go the whole hog. Ooh, yummy, that's a great choice, flicking my gaze away from staring at the Cinnamon Orange Spice tea in his basket, I pretend to examine tea accessories.

"Cin."

"Hmm?"

"C'mere a sec."

Smiling at the lady on duty, I wander back to where he's standing, "Yup?"

"We have to. Say yes."

Laughing, I nod. A mud bath just adds to the perfection of

Djinn

what we're setting out to achieve. He grins at my response and puts in a large supply of French white clay from their bathroom selection, into his basket.

"I know two people getting messy really soon. All we need now is a lot of raw honey and massage oils and we'd be complete."

He laughs softly, "That can be arranged."

I wink back when he winks at me, sneaking away to get ceremonial mandrake root and dragon's blood bath salts.

Meeting up with him again, he shows me the latest treasures.

"It's traditional to give the Shaman a gift. Look what I got."

I nod approval at the bamboo tea strainer, cotton drawstring bags, camphor crystals and echinacea tincture for the gift. We both get aloe-vera lip balm, soap and gel, arnica gel and Bob's bug off.

"Oh cool, they've got cedar wood. That'll smell great on the fire." He adds that to his growing collection of goodies.

"I'll see your cedar wood and raise you one," I grin and add cinnamon bark to my basket.

Covertly I grab the black magic woman pheromone oil and hide it under the gel.

"What's that?"

I hadn't realised he was looking over my shoulder, standing behind me.

"Pheromone oil? Hmm." He fingers a bunch of them and gives me a secret smirk, "How about some Beat-Me-Baby? Ooo! Or, Chained Desire. This stuff sounds like it should be on an edible menu."

"They'd make great names for cocktails."

He laughs and goes back to selecting charcoals and sage smudge sticks, presumably for the Shaman.

With the privacy gap I put Tantric Power pheromone incense into my basket and go to the check out.

Poppet

Finally back in the car with clothes, food, supplies, and treasures, we take the drive out to the Shaman.

"So tell me about the Shaman."

"Nope."

"Why not?"

"You've never met one have you? They don't keep friends who talk about them."

"What's his name?"

"If he tells you, he's accepted you. If he doesn't, it's not my place to share that information."

"Shees. You guys take this seriously."

"It is serious."

Leaning back, I stare at the view, "Sash –"

"Hmmm?" he rubs my thigh distractedly, still focused on the road.

"It strikes me that we're really compatible. We've got way too much in common."

"I've been trying to convince you of that for years. You only believe me now?"

The smile he's giving me could power Hong Kong for a year.

"So you were right." I concede with my own wry grin.

"If I have my way, I'm never letting you go."

"Then you're in need of a padded room. Life has been demonic since we got together."

"And magical."

I don't need a fortune teller to know what he's referring to. I pulled out all the stops to get him away from that redhead.

"Yeah well ..."

He laughs and points at the iPod.

"Pick a tune."

⛧

Djinn

 Chapter 17

Cindy:

I stand patiently, letting the long haired man wave his white sage smudge stick all around me.

"Now you may enter the inipi wickiup."

"The what?" I ask.

"The purification teepee." He looks at Sasha, "Where did you find her? Did you tell her nothing?"

"Not a thing," he says, wearing a scoundrel grin.

The Shaman nods slowly, in a thoughtful manner, then stares into my eyes with a brown gaze, "I did my training not according to our local tribes. In my way, we call this a temazcalli. It's a Nahuati word which means 'house of heat', but this is a purification Sasha requested."

"So you're not really Indian?"

His tanned face reveals nothing, "Are any of us just a label?"

Sasha offers information, "He trained in mesoamerica."

That's just as informative. I'm still clueless. Annoyed, I turn and enter the round room, partially peeved with cryptic clues and ignorance.

Idiots.

"Sit there," the Shaman says, pointing to the north.

"Why?"

"Because you're white and you like categories to put people

Poppet

into."

I give him my 'fuck you' smile and move to where he pointed, seating myself on a Peruvian looking woven rug.

He waits for Sasha to sit opposite me on the other side of the hot stones.

"Take off all jewelry."

Removing my rings I hand them over and use the opportunity to examine him. He doesn't look like anything special. Black jeans, normal shoes, collarless white shirt, and no markings or adornments. Although he looks authentically American Indian.

His hair is glorious, coating down his back to his waist, giving him a careless air. Men with long hair seem defiant. I like that.

He sits down at the entrance with a regal posture and speaks in a soothing meditative tone. "The traditional inipi has the door open to the fire outside where we collect the rocks. You are here to reflect, to heal, to let go of your anger, to examine your subconscious, and to commune with the Great Spirit."

Now he has my attention. The great spirit I can relate to.

He looks at Sasha, "You did a terrible thing Silent Foot. No one may kill a spider. You offend Kokyanwuhti."

Sasha looks down, inclining his head with silent acceptance of the rebuttal. These two speak their own silent language because Sasha picks up a handful of cherry tobacco and puts it in the stone pit. Instantly smoke writhes away in swirled reaction. Scooping a cup of scented blessed rainwater, he pours it slowly in the same place, causing the fire rocks to fizzle and hiss, a cloud of steam erupts, blurring the Shaman.

The Shaman nods with approval and Sasha settles back on his rug.

Then he looks to me, "When in the wrong, you must make a peace offering."

I stare back with a mouth full of teeth. It's getting hot in here.

Djinn

"Why are you here?"

Crap, he's looking at me.

"Uhm, it was Sasha's idea."

He turns his head, glossy black hair catches the light from beyond the door like a sliver of moonlight, "Silent Foot?"

"We need healing medicine from the Great Spirit. Death and rebirth, to start again."

Shaman nods again, looking deeply into the volcanic stone pit, as if for answers.

"When cleansing is over, you must move to eagle."

"Yes. I know."

I look insistently at Sasha, "And where is eagle?"

He gives me a naughty grin, "White skin you are impatient for answers. Why not wait and see?"

"You're white skin too," I grumble. I know he's teasing but I'm tired of the two of them speaking in riddles.

He laughs, but Shaman shuts us up by pouring more water into the pit to create a fog of steam, isolating us on our respective sides without visual contact while the hell-hot rocks hiss angrily, loud enough to drown out conversation.

"We begin," the mysterious man announces with authority.

For some reason this makes me nervous.

"Either watch the pit, or close your eyes. I will guide you now."

He snaps the door cover down and we're immediately alone in the dark with red glowing stones heating our faces like scorning eyes of judgement.

"Thukasila, Até Wakha Thaka, tonkan tatapika, hanikpaza kin, mni wakanta najin ki, pejihintanpa kin, takuxika teriya tiyoslohanhan hinyunke ..."

I zone out, staring at the volcanic rocks. They waver and dance with the heat, challenging nature and all people who say rocks do not melt; they *can* run like rivers and kill everything they touch. We wear rocks in jewelry, decorating ourselves as if we're important, yet we're nothing when the rocks come back to reclaim what we've stolen. That's real smiting. When lava runs, nothing gets away from instant karma. Why did people sacrifice virgins to volcanoes?

"... mitakuye oyas'in."

"Thank you Hukpaksica," Sasha responds at the end.

I guess I missed it. Hukpaksica?

"Is that your name?"

He stares at me like he can see my soul dancing shadows on the wall behind me, telling him secrets of revenge and lust.

"It means medicine man. A bad medicine man is Heyókha. Iktomi do bad medicine."

He gestures to Sasha, "Opági."

He complies and sprinkles the bark he brought with on the stones between us.

Shaman then looks to me, "Opági."

Playing it by ear, I sprinkle some of the cinnamon bark on the stones, virtually turning my fingertips incandescent.

He then puts the same in his pipe and lifts it up. Adopting a drum with his right hand, he begins beating it in a steady heart pump, doing the whole hay-ya-ya thing.

Stifling a laugh, I purse my lips together tightly and glare at the fire with feigned seriousness.

Sasha whispers, "Prayers," to me, in explanation, before relaxing and closing his eyes, moving with the sway of a leaf in a sirocco breath.

The heat is oppressive and I watch the dark shape on the wikiup behind Sasha, listening to the drum. It's hypnotic, focusing becomes a challenge, sweat runs into my eye and the stones periodically gasp hot steam.

I keep seeing dead trees in my mind's eye, in barren landscapes, just sand and blackened twigs, the scream long gone

Djinn

from their bark and wood. The eternal rings of life rotted out of them from the inside out. Hazy mirages cloud the red sand, leaving behind huge bones, the remnants of a carcass picked clean and bleached white by the eternal sun. The only adornment of desert are those bones, a memory of life.

Softly I hear the rattlesnake, it rattles with the drum, singing its rasping shwisper to the wind and fire. They come to the fire to drink in the heat, this is home, this is comfort.

Where did all these snakes come from?

Why isn't anyone reacting?

Looking from Sasha's unfocused stare, to the shaman who seems a long distance off, I look back at the languid snakes, unblinking, watching me.

Sasha:

Spotted Eagle picks up his rattle and begins to shake it with the beating of his drum. In the spirit lodge, rain touches my blistering skin, soothing, cooling, reminding me of the great Earth Mother who never forsakes her children.

The rattle becomes the hoof beats of the wild palomino running free, it's the corn sprinkled into the bowl to be ground for food, it is the splashing of children playing in the river, morphing to the last tear a mother cries in grief before looking up with renewed determination to walk gentle, even if none have shown her the courtesy. Melancholy sadness shrouds me with her hair, kissing my cheeks and reminding me that desolation comes before renewal. The winter before the birth, when it's coldest and the wind is harsh.

Challenges lie ahead before spring can bless where our feet walk. Nothing will bloom until we've endured the coldest part of this soul winter.

Poppet

Spotted Eagle changes the tempo and the heat rushes in at me, bringing me back to where I am. It's fevered, pushing at us in waves until we go under, swallowed by the Great Spirit, diving deep in the ecstasy of union, every beat pushing out the venom of not forgiving. Sucking all the pain from my pores like heat fleas, taking out the poison in body tears, washing away the grief of my parent's death, the fear of Cindy's poltergeists, the demon ...

Big eyes loom over me, dark and onyx black, glistening wetly. The veins in my neck pulsate painfully against asphyxiation – Graham's undead eyes – Heather screaming – Cindy laughing – planchette tap dancing over her skull in time with the spirit drum – Cindy becomes Graham, her body a skein of pain, wrung tight so blood drips slowly into a barrel from her split skin and boneless frame, screaming, it rips my sanity into prayer flags flapping in the wind, the Eagle flies to me, taking me higher, circling upward, the wind is cool, the sun cold, the glare blinding – Hold tight brother – Do not lose me – It's Jon Spotted Eagle, taking me to the summit to wash in the Great Thunder. Tension runs out through the soles of my feet like a radiator leaking anti-freeze – the color is squalid and vile, turning away, I step into the thundering white waters to be washed of guilt.

Cindy:

Lazing on a hot beach, under the bronze sun, sipping from a coconut, aquamarine water blesses my locks with shy kisses. The water inches closer and closer, staring up at sparkling diamonds raining from a blue sky, lightning dives for my legs, turning the sand instantly to glass. The clap leaves me with hair on end and panicked.

My heartbeat is loud like a drum pounding, frenzied, wild, making me breathless.

With his hair blowing in lacy wisps behind his head, the

Djinn

Shaman shows me the glass – showing me the beauty created by fire when we allow it to transform, my skin tingles and hums from the static charge and near death of lightning – the golden light turns choked black with coiling smoke, thick and suffocating, it wraps tight around me, lifting me up – carrying me like a queen of death down a long cave tunnel where only heat glows from basalt rocks, the smell overpowering like a match just lit – Graham flung against cave walls, again and again like a Ping-Pong ball, smashing to a pulp, blood spewing from his broken mouth and cracked nose – he sees me, screaming – help – dum dum dum dum – pounding drumming – loud – louder – against my head – holding it – too hot – burns – burns – book pages eddying like a snow flurry of paper – sucking me into the vortex, round and round and down and round, dizzy, stomach left behind in the plummet – going to vomit – a hand grabs mine and I look into blue eyes. So evil, so beautiful, falling ...

Snatch – yanked upward – rising fast like a shuttle, we float into orbit above a flat plain – grass billows in invisible wind, it whistles a chilling cry and the sun pulsates like a neon light – a feather points to the lake – cool – I need the cool – letting go – I drop, diving into the clear crisp water – thunder roars in my ears as bubbles swirl and dance – rattles trickle water and the cold gives me relief until they become shivers – the shivers burn – water runs over my skin in hot/cold frosting – opening my eyes – the stone pit looms carbuncle bright, a book floating above it, over the open pages I see death staring back at me. It falls into a crater with a scream loud enough to burst eardrums. Dum dum dum dum, a sure beating hand brings me back to the wikiup. I'm in two places at once, lifting my hand, I can see through it as if I've become an apparition, staring through my own skin and bone at my lover.

Sasha opens his eyes and looks deep into my heart, such beauty emanating from him like cosmic dust in a pond ripple,

Poppet

widening, floating through me in comforting rings of vibrating gold light – the drumbeat halts abruptly and the Shaman stands, flipping the door open, blinding me with daylight. Blinking rapidly, I have black spots in my vision.

He returns, coming back to give us each a clay jar of water.

"Drink slowly."

It's so cool and wet, like it was kept in a mountain stream to stay refreshing. Sasha still hasn't looked away and I feel my soul violated and kissed simultaneously.

My robe clings to me and I become aware of how saturated I am. The atmosphere in here is oppressive.

"Silent Foot, we must talk," the Shaman says in a stern voice.

Sasha breaks contact, taking his carafe and following the Shaman into the night, leaving me alone with a sense of dread and abandonment.

Inching closer to eavesdrop, I hear anger in the Shaman's voice.

"You fell off the sacred hoop. You walk the red road."

Sighing, not understanding the message at all, I close my kimono tight and take another sip.

Sasha:

He prods me in my shoulder, "Inipi, Silent Foot."

"I know. It means to strengthen the will in a sacred way."

"There's too much pain there. You choose the body over the sacred. Your hoop is now a noose and it's squeezing you brother."

"Look, can we talk about this later?"

He nods, "You must be hungry. Your cabin is ready, just take all plastic back with you."

"I know." Nodding with respect, I then slap his shoulder, "Thanks Jon. If anyone can cure her, you can."

"You think I'm the Great Spirit. I'm not. She has taken very

Djinn

bad medicine. I do not want to go where her spirit goes. It's enough to make a good man sick." He gives me his signature smile, "Now you look just like a pale face. You are afraid, you know there's something wrong." His teasing at movie-speak isn't enough to make me smile.

Staring at the ground between us, I fear he speaks the truth. Swallowing retorts, I mumble, "Time to clean up. She and I are going in there alone later."

"No. Too soon. Tomorrow rather."

Bowing my head, I respect his guidance.

"Then I'm taking her out. We need, both of us, we need to shake this curse."

"What happened?"

"An exorcist was murdered by a demon in my home."

His expression shutters me out, his posture changes, subtly, but rigidity is there. "Let me speak to the elders. We don't like your bad medicine. We do not do the things you do. Your folk go looking for trouble. You must make peace with the Spirits and heal. You can't rush this."

"Ómakiya yo makakize lo," I speak his language for privacy and out of respect.

The rattle in his hand reacts automatically, shaking to disperse the evil. "I know you are suffering Sasha. I will help you if I can. You know I will try."

Uncomfortable, I turn back to the sweat lodge to get Cindy after giving him the best gratitude expression I can muster.

She sits staring into space, "I'm going to our cabin to shower."

"Okay," is all she says, staying where she is.

Shrugging, feeling the cold of the air now, I move toward our log cabin, suddenly tired.

Poppet

Cindy:

Once I know Sasha's gone, I crawl over to the door and stare at the Shaman. He stares back.

Like whispering a secret, he says, "Okáwjge. What you do comes back to you."

He blends into the darkness, like a tree that has always been here, a sentry keeping watch over the years, witnessing our triumphs and failings.

"Wa'úsila wachatognake. You must pity good hearted people." His voice should hold accusation, but it doesn't. "You are selfish. That is why you have this problem." He ends the discussion by turning and walking toward the main house.

He stops halfway, looking back at me, "Do you celebrate thanksgiving?"

"Who doesn't?"

He points to his chest, "In here. Thanksgiving with your heart. Wóphila."

I am compelled to answer truthfully. He has the strangest effect on me.

"No."

"Sasha is chaté t'jza. But I do not think he is brave enough for both of you."

"What does that even mean? Why don't you just speak English? This is America. You don't impress me with your fancy words."

"It means he is a brave heart." His gaze becomes piercing, like dark pins in the cosmos. "You walk on my land. I do not walk on yours."

I can tell I've offended him because he turns and points away while taking the worn path to his home, "Walk the medicine wheel."

I look across at a pile of stones in a circle which he indicated.

Djinn

Fuck that.

Sasha:

Standing alone in the moonlight, I listen to him in the wikiup.

"Wayagkhiya yo. Wayagkhiya yo. Chanupa ki le wakhá yelo. Wayagkhiya yelo he haaa."

I am ashamed. Looking at the brushed ground, it's instinct to translate it. He is praying for us, beseeching the spirits.

Look at this. Look at this. This pipe is sacred. Look at this.

Oh Jon, I am so sorry I made my problems your problem.

He comes rushing out of the wikiup. "It was a hobo spider!"

How did he even know I was here? When he does stuff like this it freaks me out. He leaves me in no doubt the Great Spirit speaks directly to him.

"Yes. How did you know?"

"Hobomok. The one you call the Devil. It was his message, his claim, his mark. Turn away from her Sasha. You cannot save her."

"But, what if it's all my fault and I'm the only one who can undo this? I am responsible Shaman. This is all my fault."

"How can it be your fault?" he asks, pointing the rattle at me, his chest and muscular arms glistening in the warping moonlight.

It occurs to me that he was overdressed earlier with a woman present, following the old tradition of propriety with mixed sexes in an inipi.

"I'm the one who accidentally smeared her blood in the pages of that book. If I hadn't put her on the bed, none of this would have happened."

Meeting gaze to gaze, the moon blacks out, and in an instant I've lost him. It judges me, showing me how I've lost my way and plunged us into the realm of the undead, where no light shines.

Poppet

Even my guide cannot go there. We are alone in this darkness. Desolation withers me.

Djinn

Chapter 18

Sasha:

I feel human again. Rolling over, I notice it's at least midday and Cindy is missing. Sitting up, her nimble frame perches on a chair in shadow.

"What time is it?"

"Time to wake up."

Moving closer to see her, I observe the dark rings and pallor of her face, "Didn't you sleep well?"

"I can't sleep."

"What do you mean you can't sleep?"

"I'm agitated all the time. Nervous, as if I'm in trouble, or something big and unpleasant is coming."

"It's part of the cleansing. Sometimes letting go of what wounds you is harder than you might think."

"I'm also craving a steak rare enough to make the blood run."

"It's vegetarian only for the purification, you know that."

"I know."

Her voice is tinged with resentment.

"I'm not going through this alone. Cindy, this is important, for both of us."

Her eyes narrow, and I only now spot her hair is wet and her skin is powdered with perspiration.

"Are you feeling ill?"

Poppet

"Let's just get this over with so we can go home," she says, standing and moving to the cabin door, flinging it wide and moving like a silkie into the sunlight.

Still half asleep, I make my way to the bathroom.

Sasha:

"Where is she?" Jon Spotted Eagle asks me in the kitchen.

"Probably down at the river. She's becoming resistant."

"Hobomok thinks he owns her. He nests and multiplies in her skin."

Finishing breakfast, I take a sip of tea. "What do you suggest?"

"Destroy the vessel. It's the only way to break the connection and hold over her."

"The last person who tried to do that ended up dead."

"And you have guilt over that. But it was their choice, not yours."

"I know, it doesn't make me feel any better."

"The stones are ready, take her in again, convince her to let him go."

I nod, "Thanks Jon. You're a life saving shaman."

"The Spotted Eagle won't be there to rescue you this time. Trust the Spirit."

"Is it my fault?"

"You love her, you seek to impress, you could not know what it was you gave her."

"And my home, and the dice?"

"She owns the dice. She carries them on her at all times."

"She does?"

"Yes. She uses them when you sleep, they induce a trance and she says things she does not understand. She is cursing my land, Sasha. Today you must leave."

Djinn

Breakfast now leaves a residue which makes me bilious. There's too much going on that I have no clue about. So she doesn't sleep because she's ... what? Possessed? She's his new vessel?

"You already know the answers, ask me no further. Have your sweat and go."

He has to be psychic. Or my aura is as easy to read as a comic book.

"Thank you for everything, Jon."

"Inipi, do not forget the In of Inipi."

I nod, "The spirit and the breath. Breathing it in, breathing it out, yes."

"Complete the rebirth and move to eagle."

I bow marginally, to thank him, leaving the security and comfort of his home and going to find the troubled soul who walks the path of complicity.

I find her at the stream, standing ankle deep, staring sightlessly at the water.

She doesn't look my way at all when she speaks, showing no indication she knew I was here, "It shows me things. Good things."

"Scrying is an ancient form of divination and fortune telling. The water was the first mirror used for sight-seeing."

Haunted eyes look up, troubled and afraid, "I'm scared."

Offering her my hand, I encourage, "Come. One more sweat, then we can go."

She nods, taking my hand and tiptoeing over river stones to the sand. Snaking an arm around my waist, she leans heavily against me, pausing us under the dappled shadows of a tree, "Sasha, you mean a lot to me. I just need you to know that."

Staring back into her eyes, I reassure her, "Likewise."

Leading her back to the lodge, I get her settled and then take the hot volcanic rocks from the fire and carry them to the pit.

Poppet

Moving in, closing the flap, I sit next to her this time, pouring water onto the rocks, offering tobacco and fragrant leaves, closing my eyes and speaking silently to the Great Spirit, asking for us to be removed now, completely, from all evil influences.

Pouring more water, I glance her way, to see her staring sightlessly into the ethereal glowing steam. Jon Spotted Eagle begins drumming outside at the fire, giving us the path to follow to the totem and guide. Knowing he's there is silent reassurance. I offer tobacco for him too, just for good measure.

"What is the red road?"

Startled from my reverie, my hand still on the tobacco pouch, I look at her glistening face, "The path to war."

"We are going to war?"

"Yes."

She looks back at the glowing rocks in the pit, dismissing me as if she hadn't spoken. Maybe she didn't. Maybe I imagined it.

"Do you think trepanning works?" she says.

"No. Drilling a hole in your head has to be the dumbest idea mankind's come up with yet."

"I feel like I've been through it. My headache is smack in the middle of my forehead above my eyebrows."

Splashing more water onto the stones, I listen to the drumming which seems louder and more insistent. "Just focus on your will. We're here to make your will stronger, connecting your spirit with the Great Spirit, tempering you like a steel blade which overcomes anything in combat."

"Have you seen Kill Bill?"

I look at her profile which stares at the pit, "Definitely. It kicks ass."

"I'd like a sword like that. I wish we really could kill people and get away with it like they did in that movie."

Hang on.

"Are you saying you feel the urge to murder?"

Djinn

"Don't pretend you've never wished someone dead."

"I've never wished someone dead. That's just wrong."

"I wished Heather and Graham dead. One down, one to go."

"Why? What did they ever do to you?"

"It's the way she touches you and talks down to me. Insinuating manipulative bitch."

Looking away from her, it's the first time I become aware of the whirring. I nudge Cindy.

"Are you seeing what I'm seeing?"

"Dancing shadows."

"Running, like we're in the middle of a hurricane funnel. But check it out, they're human looking."

"Want to know what I think is weird? Those shadows come from in here. The light source is in here. But we can only see the shadows, not the things making them."

"Where are the dice?"

My jaw locks when the circling shadows stop with my words and look our way. Silhouettes of monsters loom large on the high walls.

"What dice?" she replies innocently.

Is she a pathological liar?"

"The divination dice."

"The ones Djinn gave me?"

"Yes."

"How do you know I have them?"

"I have my sources."

She turns and stares at me, adjusting her entire position so she remains facing me instead of the pit.

"Why do you want them?"

"I don't. I just don't think it's a good idea for you to use them. They summon bad things, Cindy. You're flirting with things you don't understand."

"And you do?"

Poppet

"There's always a consequence, for every action."

"Are you judging me?"

"No. I'm giving you spiritual counsel."

The shadows begin beating their astral fists into the walls. The drum reverberates through the room as if it's a gong above our heads, puffing air at us with each 'dum'.

"I don't like this."

"Face your demons Cindy. They're all yours."

"I don't have demons."

"Yes you do, all seventy-two of them."

"Go to hell."

"Look around you, we're already there. I have chosen to see your spirit along with you. What we're looking at is the legion fighting you for your skin suit and your soul."

Tilting her head back she unleashes a scream that belongs in Hollywood.

My entire body crawls with reaction, and to his credit, Jon continues his drumming outside.

"What the fuck did you do that for?" I ask, unnerved. And definitely with a large dose of pissed off on the side.

"Tension release. I'm terrified out of my mind."

"You don't look terrified out of your mind."

She glares at me, "I have a very hard time revealing emotion."

"Why don't you like Heather?"

"She judged me and wants you. She thinks she's God's golden child. She's not."

"She's twice my age."

"So? There are plenty of cougars roaming the nights these days."

"It takes two."

"What did she do in your car?" she interrupts me with accusation thick in her tone.

Djinn

"Nothing."

"Liar."

"I'm not lying, Cin."

"Then why the change in your attitude after?"

"Because you were floating on the ceiling speaking like a ratchet with your eyes rolled back in your head, and it scared the crap out of me."

"I – what?"

Even in this dim light I can see how white her face has become.

"When you bled all over Djinn."

"Why didn't you tell me?"

"How? How do you tell the girl you have designs on that she's Satan's puppet?"

"If you loved me you would have told me!"

"Where are the dice?"

Her eyes glimmer and a tension so tight and terrifying gives my eyebrows their own erection, standing out dead straight, while I wait for her counter-spirit to confront me. She surprises me and instead hands over a bag from her pocket.

Opening it up, I pour out eleven stones.

"Where's the twelfth?"

She folds her arms, defiant. The shadows blur into a black mist, becoming so agitated they're intimidating. I can feel their presence in here pushing against our backs.

"Give me the twelfth one, Cindy."

Her hand worms out and drops the last one into my hand with a click. The drumming is fevered, the air around us visibly pulsating, the heat blurring clear vision with humidity and vapors swirling like Draco circling the night sky.

Without hesitation, I deposit all of the stones directly onto forge hot volcanic rocks. They dance like popcorn and Cindy somersaults backwards across the floor squealing like a sacrifice.

Poppet

Snapping back with natural reflex I grab onto her wrist, holding her from being snatched by shadows all playing tug of war with me on the wall behind us. It reminds me of an old black and white pantomime, except this is a fight for her life, for her soul.

Leaning back, it's taking all my strength to hold onto her, her hands slipping with the heat induced moisture coating both of us like wrestling oil, her arms outstretched, her body mid-air, gritting her teeth in a snarl, there's pure fear in her eyes.

"Hang on."

She unleashes another vertebrae shattering scream and my soul clenches in response. Yanking her back, deliberately covering her with my weight and forcing us both to lie flat on the woven floor, I shield her while the air screeches and tornadoes, blustering wind whips up the rugs and a fearful howling bellows around us.

The darkness in here is so thick now, I can't see the glowing stones. An icy dread grips me while a powerful horror works around us, cocooning us into its wicked silk, separating us from the living.

Automatically I throw a cup of water on the stones with one arm, correctly guessing their location, maintaining my limpet position over Cindy, praying for help and deliverance when the rocks send up steam prayers to God.

She wriggles beneath me like Houdini hanging upside down in a straitjacket. I hold her tight until the shadows fade and we're alone again with glowing stones and sweat.

The rattle shakes and I hear the singing coming faintly through the unnatural calm. In here it's hard to tell what's real and what's not. Everything we just went through could have been completely in the spirit realm.

Daring to look down, her eyes are squeezed shut with tears spitting out, shaking like an epileptic with sobs.

Djinn

Holding her now in a relaxed embrace, I give her hugging comfort.

Time warps along with consciousness, because I recall nothing, yet now she's sitting on me wearing a suicidal smile.

God that feels good.

Forgetting the maelstrom of evil, I surrender to a living fantasy.

Closing my eyes against the demented expression masking her face, what I see isn't real, it's just a remnant still circulating in here from the dark manifestation earlier.

Choosing instead to indulge my senses in the euphoric pleasure caused by her warm body, I send out my spirit to watch instead, the way Jon taught me. He said the spirit always walks ahead of you, knowing what's coming, and that two people cannot meet until their spirits have first interacted and agreed on the meeting being mutually acceptable, keeping the body safe from harm.

Watching, I question my vision. Instead of her hourglass shape, I can see broad shoulders and muscular arms. Flicking channels, I open my eyes to engage in physical vision again; she's back, petite and petal precious. I smile at her, gazing into eyes which are oddly sea green in this lighting.

She smiles back, and I close my eyes again, hoping Jon stays out of here while I'm alone with my girl, doing what lovers do when they're alone in a sweat lodge.

Poppet

 Chapter 19

Sasha:

Leaving all of my supplies at Jon's as a gift of silent thanks, I direct the Honda to Breitenbush Hot Springs.

After we closed the ceremony with the four directions. I took the time to explain it to her.

"North is White Buffalo, representing the white skinned people, adulthood, body, plants and animals. It can represent birth. East is for Asian and Polynesian people, we call it eagle. It represents death and rebirth. South represents childhood, we call the direction Serpent. It holds the heart, red skinned people, and fire. West is the final stage of the wheel, it is spirit, water, and blue or black skinned people. We call the direction Bear."

"Why can't you just call it by its cardinal name?"

"Honour the customs of the people you go to for help, Cindy. Be humble and respectful."

"It's not in my nature to be either."

Shooting a glance at her being far too quiet in the passenger seat, I tempt her out of her shell.

"Are you going to join me for a hot stone massage?"

"We never used the clay."

Djinn

She sounds disappointed and almost accusatory.

"We can now."

"Did you book?"

"Yes ma'am. I booked a cabin."

"And champagne?"

"No, we're still on our purification binge."

"I'm dying for a smoke."

"That's allowed in the old tradition if it's done as an offering."

She gives me a quick smile, leaning forward and extracting the box from the glove compartment.

"Pull over. Let's hide away and have a smoke."

I do as she asks, stopping the car in a glade of trees off to the side of the road, with enough privacy for us not to get spotted by any passing vehicles, and am rewarded with a lingering kiss and intimate staring before she tugs my hand and opens her door.

After an afternoon of deep tissue massage, basalt stone massage, reflexology, Lomi Lomi and Shiatsu, I'm a puddle of relaxed. I think I'm de-evolving into an amoeba.

Sitting opposite her in the cabin, we indulge in feeding each other organic delicacies off their menu to replenish our flagging appetites. I bought her a turquoise pendant, explaining to her the Hopi creation myth of how Spider Woman created hard woman with her stones. I'm hoping the protection of this ancient native stone will keep her safe after all we've been through. And right now it's all she's wearing.

There's an odd companionship and peace between us, which is new. We've always had an undercurrent of tension, and it's blissfully missing.

Slathering each other in white clay, we relax in the warm bathroom which we've turned into our own private steam room, allowing the clay to purify us further, taking us the rest of the way to rebirth.

I wonder who's phoned? Two days without being able to switch on a cell phone has been liberating. They're forbidden here too; the world can wait until we leave.

Washing off clay in needles of shower water, it's as if we've been a couple for years. We've certainly lived through more than most couples do in a lifetime.

This is why we like being called a couple and why we yearn for relationships. Skin intimacy, having the freedom to sponge clay off a lover's back, pressing closely together in the confines of a shower, these are the experiences which humanize us.

It feels good on multiple levels of the body and psyche. It feels, 'home'.

It is home.

Exhausted, I snuggle her warm body next to mine on the double bed, choosing to sleep until I wake. That's the best part of a holiday, taking the time to catch up on much needed sleep.

Waking at twilight the following day, I get to wake her with organic coffee, relieved she's sleeping.

"We've slept all day," I whisper to her barely conscious form.

"And we can screw all night."

The way she answers quickly, half awake, I love this about her. She inches up, cradling the cup, inhaling appreciatively.

I grin back at her impish smile and wild white hair, "I was thinking we could take a moonlit walk through the labyrinth before heading to the Villa Kitchen."

"I suggest we have food first, followed with a moonlit walk, then we go to the sauna, ending it with wallowing in the silent pools."

"Deal."

The connection is stronger, the peace deeper; this is me living the dream.

Djinn

The dream becomes perfection, holy, sanctified, washed in secretive rays from a white moon reflecting off the steaming water in the silent pool. We maintain the silence, using water ripples to communicate. It's like being with a twin in a womb, fluid runs lazy fingers over oversensitive hair follicles, snaking out hair in kelp undulations when we go under the water, truly ending our rebirth with apt imagery.

Moving up to take a life enhancing breath of clean air, she breaches the water, tilting and smoothing her hair back. I wish I could paint. I'd capture this forever.

She looks purer than Madonna with the way the white light glosses her wet skin, shiny shapes emerge, and I half expect to see Venus raise up higher, teasing me with a clam shell.

I'm too choked to speak, instead I stare, etching this moment into my soul.

It's an anticlimax heading home the next morning. We've both completely ignored our responsibilities this week. Spiritual warfare has a way of doing that to you, but now I have to face my home, ready or not.

"Are you sure you want me to drop you at home?"

She nods, vacantly caressing a hand over my thigh, "Yes. I need to catch up with Rachel. Want to come over later for fondue or something?"

"Love to."

Stopping to fill up with gas, I take a walk into the store to stock up on smokes too.

Cindy:

The minute he's out of sight I switch his phone on. I've

Poppet

memorized the password, and quickly put it in.

I knew it!

Deleting all the missed calls and messages from Heather Black, I switch it off and hide it back where he left it.

With my loving face on, I watch him when he saunters back toward the car looking like a surfer returning from Hawaii. He has an air of meditative relaxation about him. Like a narcotic you just can't get enough of.

He has a good soul. He's a good guy. I wish I'd figured that out years ago. Fingering the turquoise stone between my breasts, I gift him with a smile when the door opens.

I wait for him to drive away, watching him from my window, but he fiddles with his phone and makes calls. He's phoning her, I know he is.

I hate her!

Fed up, I stomp to get Djinn.

Sasha:

The only calls I have are from Jerry. I'm glad he called, I could use the back up. Waiting patiently I stare out of the open window at the quiet street.

"Jerry, Sash. Sorry man, I had my phone off." - "We went to the Shaman." - "Haha, yeah I got freaked out and left the door open. Thanks for closing it. Listen, I have to go back in and wondered if you felt like coming over to help me spring clean. The sign has to come down ..." - "Cool. Thanks dude. Spot you in five."

Happy now, I take a quick drive to TJ's to stock up again before meeting Jerry at home.

He's waiting outside when I pull up. Getting out with my parcels,

Djinn

I head for the front door.

"So what happened?"

"I called the Phantom Professionals, and one of them died in here."

"Shit. That's pretty heavy."

"You're telling me."

I open the door and stare inside. It's dark and quiet.

"It's your home, walk in and own it."

I give him a smile, "Thanks for having my back."

My intestines are in a knot and I'm tense, but take five steps in regardless, waiting for the shit to hit the jet engine.

Nothing happens.

Suspicious, I take the stuff to the kitchen and start stocking the fridge.

Jerry follows me in, staring out the window. "I heard salt works."

"I thought that was a myth?"

He shrugs, "Doesn't hurt to try."

Nodding, I extract the salt from the pantry and start sprinkling it around.

"I need to check the bedroom. The door apparently unhinged itself and shoved Graham down the stairs."

He looks serious when I expected him to laugh, "And you believe that?"

"I don't know what to believe any more."

He grabs a knife from the butcher's block and walks with me to the stairs. They creak as we ascend, halting we stare into the bedroom.

"It looks normal."

"And that's what bothers me," I say. "When we left it was in a hurry. Do you know any demons that clean up?"

"Only elves," he laughs.

I appreciate the levity, and scatter salt while taking the steps into my haven with trepidation. Surveying everything with diligence, I go over to the window and push it up. Inspecting it for scores in the paint where it could catch and scream, looking for evidence of broken glass. Staring down I can still see blood in the geraniums below, but that's the only sign that something untoward ever happened.

Ducking back in, I look under the bed.

"Nothing strange here, dude. It feels a little weird, like it's been unlived in for too long, but otherwise I'd say the coast is clear."

I agree with Jerry, but he's watching me closely.

"Yeah, up here looks okay. Wanna help me clear out the shop?"

"But that's your income."

"It's time for me to find a new income."

"That's a bit extreme, don't you think?"

"No. I never want to sell a book like Djinn again."

He nods, "Okay."

Without hesitation he heads for the stairs. Sighing, looking around again, I make my way downstairs, opening the shutters and windows, encouraging life back into the sarcophagus.

It takes us no longer than an hour to dump it all in rubbish bags and fill the outside trash bins. Getting the sign down was tricky, and we finally stand on either side like inspectors over an exhumed body.

I hold up a hand, "Hang on, give me two secs." Running in, I retrieve two golf clubs from the hall closet. Returning, I hand him one, "Give it everything you've got."

Slamming the nine iron into the perspex dice, I shatter it, releasing rage and anxiety with every clubbing I deliver.

Jerry seems just as intent on mayhem, delivering expert blows to the frame, breaking its bones in multiple fractures.

"Glad you're not my enemy," I grunt at him between exerted

Djinn

heaves.

"If this sign pissed you off this much, I'm happy to put it into an early grave."

Laughing, swinging wildly, we share an exchange over the wide box, grinning like two teenagers up to no good.

Staring at carnage, he drops the iron, wiping his hair out of his eyes, "Now what?"

"Bonfire."

"Awesome!"

"Doctor, lighter fluid, stat."

"Yes doctor," he hands the fluid to me, igniting the blow torch in his left hand. "Cauterizing initiated."

We laugh, setting flame to my past, delivering me from evil and liberating my future.

Chapter 20

Cindy:

"What do you need me to do?" he asks.

"Nothing. Maybe when Raych gets here you can pour her a drink,"

"What are we drinking?"

"Red wine," I say with a smug smile.

"That smells good, what is it?" he winks, obviously enjoying teasing me.

"Chilli con carne."

"My lord, the woman can cook too."

Smacking his arm, I move to stir the pot. "Be good or I won't serve you."

"Hang on, I think my ears are blocked. Did you just say you'll serve me?"

He's laughing at me and my cheeks react by getting hotter.

"Oh just shut up and put music on or something."

He listens and moves to the CD player in the lounge.

"So did you have many messages on your phone?" I pry.

"Only from Jerry. He helped me clean house today."

"You should have invited him for dinner."

Sasha looks up, a CD case in one hand, flicking long sandy hair away from his face, "Seriously? He'd love that."

"Yeah, call him, it's not too late."

Djinn

He unearths his phone, and I pry further, "So, no word from the Blacks?"

"Nope." He puts the phone to his ear and perches on the coffee table next to Djinn, gray eyes staring intently at me with worry, "Is that weird? Should I call her?"

"Nah, if she needs you she'll call," I say casually, putting more damiana into the pot. It's a natural aphrodisiac that works like an A-bomb. As long as he's satisfied, he won't stray. Djinn said so. If I'm any kind of witch, I'm a kitchen witch.

"Dude! Dinner!"

I listen to his relaxed laugh and am immediately pleased I suggested inviting his friend. Their conversation is short and sweet, looking at his smile and sparkling eyes, a tug of affection grips me and I'm mildly ashamed for being so suspicious. If he didn't want to be with me, he wouldn't be here.

Long firm arms wrap around me and a kiss is placed on my neck, "And what would the chef like to drink?"

"Something potent."

He gives me a squeeze before releasing me and looking in the fridge.

"Hazelnut vodka?"

"Okay," I nod, turning the heat down and getting the bowls ready.

Sasha:

Jerry arrives first, bringing sherry as his offering to the chef.

"Thanks. Make yourself at home," Cindy says to him.

He plonks himself down on a chair in the lounge, picking up her guitar and playing the first chords to Stairway to Heaven."

"You do know that's the most played song by anyone learning guitar?" I tease him.

"Never mess with perfection, dude."

"Wine?"

"Yeah, okay."

Moving back to the kitchen, I pick up the first bottle we have open, it's been breathing for thirty minutes and should be perfect.

"Once, one of my idiot friends put tequila in my wine. It's the vilest drink I've ever had," Cindy shares while putting out spoons and napkins.

I pour us each a glass while Jerry answers.

"Try a vomit. Nothing beats that for gross. It congeals in your mouth."

Interrupting the music and chatter, the doorbell rings. Handing Jerry his wine on my way to the door, I open it to Rachel and Derrick.

"Greeting earthlings. Welcome to planet Chili."

They laugh and split up immediately, Rachel moving to the kitchen with bottles and desert while Derrick plants himself in a chair and eyes the TV.

"Who's watching the game?"

Falling into host shoes, I leave Jerry to fend the question, "Wine, Derrick?"

"Spot," he says in confirmation.

Walking back to the open plan kitchen, Cindy leaves, going to the bedroom with an irate expression.

Now what?

Pouring the two of them wine, I hand out the glasses and go off to the bedroom.

"Hey babes, what's up?"

She's staring in her mirror, scowling.

"What did she have to bring him for?"

"They're a couple. Didn't you invite both of them?"

"Why can't a girl just have her friend over? Why does she just assume it's always both of them?"

Djinn

"I doubt she did it to deliberately piss you off."

She flounces to her bed and sits on it with aggression.

"Now I can't tell her anything. He's such a fucking nerd. Watch, if you say two words about the spirit lodge he'll start sprouting biblical crap at you."

"So we just won't say anything."

"That's not the point!" she shouts at me.

"Honey, I think you're overreacting."

"Typical male. Stick up for him just because he has balls."

"I'm not sticking up for –"

She stalks out of the room, leaving me staring after her, wondering how she can go from relaxed and congenial to warfare pissed off, in minutes.

Walking back to help in the kitchen, hoping to keep the peace, I'm just in time to catch the drama.

"Is this that magic book you told us about?" Rachel leans over and pulls Djinn to the edge of the table.

Cindy bullets between them, pushing Djinn back, "Don't touch it."

"Why not? It's gorgeous, how old is it?"

"It's mine. I don't want your energy interfering with it."

"It's not a crystal Cin, it's just a book."

"It's not just a book!"

The rest of us are observing the interaction and experiencing the murderous tension. Jerry shifts uncomfortably and shoots me a 'what the fuck' glance. I shrug in response.

"Did you come here just to mess with my stuff?" she glares at Rachel.

"I'm here because you invited me."

"Exactly! I invited **you**! So what is **he** doing here?"

Derrick sits up straight, "I didn't realise it was an exclusive invitation."

"Neither did I," Rachel spits bitterly.

Poppet

Cindy ignores him and continues staring down at her best friend, "For once can you be an adult and do something without your warden?"

"What the hell is your problem?" Rachel's voice rises.

"He's my problem. Since you've become a permanent couple you can't do anything without him. Sometimes I need my best friend without the chaperone!"

"A friend accepts it when they have someone they love that they want to share stuff with, including their best friend. Cindy! Listen to yourself. This isn't you."

"Oh yeah, well if you don't like it you can just fuck off."

Derrick stands and towers over her, "I'm game for that suggestion. I had no idea you felt this way."

"You wouldn't have an idea. You're too thick to take a hint."

Rachel and Jerry stand with perfect synchronization.

"I should go too," Jerry says.

Cindy turns and points a finger at him, "Sit down!"

Jerry gulps at me and sits back down while Cindy waits for Rachel and Derrick to leave, which they do without saying two words.

The silence is choking me despite the music playing.

The second the door closes, she turns to me with a smile, "She won't be doing that again in a hurry."

"Cin, that's how you lose friends."

"Who needs friends like that? If she can't do anything without the penis, she's not welcome here anyway."

"That was an epic fail. I can't believe you just did that."

"Well I did, get over it."

And without another word she goes back to the kitchen.

Sinking down on the chair next to Jerry, I whisper, "Sorry man."

His gaze wanders to the book, looking back at me, he indicates it with a nudge of his head.

Djinn

I nod, giving him the 'what can I do' shrug.

Cindy:

Thirsty, I switch the light on and get out of bed. Dawdling sleepily down the passage I nearly have an aneurism seeing Sasha sitting in the lounge in the dark.

"Jesus! What are you doing in here? You half scared me to death."

His eyes have the strangest expression, his mouth is tilted unhappily while he holds his knees. "What do you think?"

"What's that supposed to mean?"

"No apology, nothing? Are you just going to pretend nothing happened?" he says.

"What the hell are you talking about?"

He stands and moves so fast to halt in front of me, it makes me instantly intimidated. Watching his face with apprehension, I notice a gash on his cheek.

Automatically lifting a hand to touch it, I ask, "Ow. What happened? Had too much wine and suffered head trauma when you kissed the floor?"

He grips my arms, fingers biting into my skin. "You're the head trauma."

"What?"

His hands are shaking, and it's giving me tension and nauseating fear. He pushes me away into the wall, showing me his arms, covered in scratches. "You did this to me, and you think you can just ignore it? I at least expect an apology. You're really something else."

He looks sick, like he's sucking on a cyanide bonbon. He's pale and it's obvious he hasn't slept but has been up all night brooding in my lounge.

Poppet

"Sasha, I don't know what you're talking about. The last thing I remember was us in the kitchen."

"Is that how you clear your conscience?"

He turns, snatching up his shirt from the back of a chair and pulling it on. There are red welts down his back too.

Shit.

Saying nothing to me, he leaves with accusation in his eyes. Accusation and a lot of hurt.

But - I didn't do anything.

Djinn

 Chapter 21

Cindy:

I have an overwhelming feeling of dread eating at me. Maybe I got drunk and don't remember? Maybe it **was** me?

Naked, I run out the door after him, calling frantically, "Sasha! Sash!"

He pops back to look up the stairwell. "For Christ's sake, Cindy. Put some clothes on."

"No."

Bursting into tears, I'm so afraid I'm about to lose him. I slide down to stare through the bars of the banister, "I'm sorry. I don't remember. Please don't leave like this."

I'm quaking unnaturally, like my soul has a fever. "I'm sorry!"

He covers the distance in moments with his long legs, "Please go inside."

"No, not unless you come in with me."

His expression is disapproving, but he wraps a warm arm around me and guides me back inside and shuts the door. "Do you have no shame?"

"You left, I couldn't just let you go."

"Just tell me why? Why would you attack me like that?"

Trembling, my knees cave, "I don't know." Wiping my eyes, sniffing, I'm shocked and afraid. "I don't remember any of it."

"That's what cowards say."

Poppet

"It's the truth! Sasha, I don't remember attacking you."

"Do you remember bitching at Rachel and making her and Derrick so uncomfortable they left?"

"What?"

He sits down in the dark, sinking into the cushions of the chair closest to me, "What **do** you remember?"

"You and me in the kitchen." Frowning, scouring my memory, I can't recall a thing from that moment. "You kissed me, I felt happy. You were going to pour vodka." Staring at him, needing him to believe me, "Sasha, what else happened? Oh God. This can't be good."

Crawling over, I take his hand, holding it to my cheek and staring at the marks on his inner forearm. "Why? Why would I do this?" Looking into his emotional eyes I have pangs of uneasiness, "What did you do? Are you sure it was me?"

He stands again, "I'm going home. I'm too tired to deal with this shit now."

"No!" Terror at being abandoned grips me and I lunge for him, the tears unchecked and torrenting down my cheeks, hot and stinging, "Please Sasha. I'll make it better."

"How?" He looks away, over my head. "No one has ever said such ghastly things to me. You went wild and now conveniently have amnesia. Crappy save Cindy. If you want me back, you'll have to do better than that."

"I don't remember! I swear!"

"Goodnight. I'll see you around."

I don't stop him this time. He doesn't look back when he leaves, closing the door softly behind him.

It's her fault!

He's looking for excuses to break up with me. She probably cursed us both so we wouldn't remember, and **she** did that to him.

And Rachel? What could I do that would make my best-friend-forever not love me?

Djinn

Nothing.
He's lying.
They're all lying!
Ganging up on me.
I'll show them. Two can play that game.

I don't care at all what other people think, or what stories they make up.

Going back to bed, I huff over and fall asleep without another thought his way. When I wake up, it's with a renewed sense of determination. Sasha is my guy. If anyone was born for me, he was. Picking up the gift certificate for burlesque lessons, I get ready to go and learn things that will twist his libido into a complicated circuit that can handle high voltage.

And after this I'm going to convince him to go out with me tonight.

Sasha:

It's changed. It's not my home any longer. Every creak makes me sweat. None of the noises are familiar, and they all have me sneaking around with a baseball bat. It's with relief that I view the sunrise streaking her optimistic rays across a cold sky.

There's only one thing for it, it's time to move.

I think I'll move to eagle, permanently, not just in the inipi.

After showering and dressing, I make the call, waiting for her, pacing like an attorney before the jury.

Sibyl arrives at thirteen minutes to nine, walking the path to my door looking every inch the professional.

Opening the door before she knocks, I offer the blond a smile, "Hi, Sybil Smith right?"

"Sasha, how do you do. So nice to meet a new client." She offers a hand and I shake it.

Poppet

"Come on in, let me show you around."

After giving her the tour, I make us coffee, and we sit opposite each other at the kitchen counter.

"May I ask why you're in such a hurry to sell?" she asks.

"Too many memories. Sometimes you just have to start over."

"Which area are you thinking of moving to? What sort of home are you looking for?"

"I'd like something a little less central, closer to nature, less traffic, bright, light and cheerful."

"Would you consider moving to Happy Valley? It has some great trails, is close to Mount Hood, and offers twenty-four acres of wetlands, but also offers you the convenience of nearby shopping and restaurants."

"I'm always open to new ideas. We can take a look," I smile.

"Your home is perfect for a couple that approached me a few days ago. If we can find you a replacement in the next few days, this sale should go through quickly."

Her words have a beam of sunshine attached directly to my aorta, heating me from the inside. "I like the name Happy Valley."

"Are you busy? Shall we go and take a look? I have a few listings you can look at."

Standing from the kitchen stool, I give her the smile I'm feeling, "Let's do it."

It's not far, but it's far enough. Happy Valley is on the other side of the 205 freeway. When we stop outside a newly built house on SE Evening Star Drive, the names click like puzzle pieces. Evening Star in Happy Valley, it's destiny, I can feel it.

Following her around the three-bedroomed house, it's perfect and I am ready to sign on the dotted line without viewing other houses.

"You're incredibly fortunate. Because it's a brand new house without previous ownership, you can probably pay occupational rent until the sale goes through, as it's got all the certificates and

Djinn

code approvals already."

Giving her my little boy smile, I say, "As long as I can move in today, I'm happy to pay rent."

"It won't be an issue, let me just make a call."

Driving back to Mountain Gate road, she takes me home. I am reborn. After days in hell, I'm ready to let the past go and move on.

Opening the front door and letting her in to my old home, I escort her to the kitchen again to put the kettle on, exchanging an excited smile.

"Sybil, I can't thank you enough. There's just one other thing about this move I need to talk to you about."

"Yes?"

"I don't plan on taking any of my belongings. I'm starting again from scratch. Do you think the new owners will want any of this?"

"Let them decide. If we have to move anything out we'll simply call the Salvation Army to recycle and reuse the items you don't want to take with you."

"Great!"

Cindy:

Prepared, I wait for him to get home. He doesn't even notice me he's so caught up in the blond.

Wow. That didn't take long. Does he have a list of women just queued up waiting in reserve for his phone call?

Bastard.

Starting the Mini, I make for home, so bitter my jaw's aching when my teeth squeak together. I'm not giving up that easy. So he

Poppet

likes the homely types does he? I'll give him homely.

Stomping up the stairs and into my kitchen, I don't pause as I get busy making chocolate chip cookies laced with more damiana.

Sasha:

Completing the paperwork and giving her my spare set of keys, I'm not worried about the money. I have tons to get done between now and nightfall because I have zero intention of spending another night here.

I head off to do some serious retail damage with shopping for a new bed, linen, drapes, towels, everything really, I consider how magical my new home is. The street is perfect. Large well tended gardens line a new smooth tarmac pavement just perfect for skateboarding. The homes are big and new, as most of them were built in the last eight years. Situated close to the corner of North Star Drive, I'm euphoric.

Bounding out of the zooty Honda, I head for Natural Spaces to get organic, natural fiber, bedding, selecting easy cream for light and tranquil, including throws and duvets. When I leave I'm overloaded with Egyptian cotton towels, organic soaps, a cobalt glass bath set, soaprocks and recycled glass dinnerware.

Now to get a king sized futon and food, and I'll be set at least for the first night in Happy Valley. Calling Organics-to-you, I place an order to have supplies delivered to me in an hour.

I feel like I've been around the world in sixty minutes when I return to Happy Valley with a car packed with new clothes from Tinctoria Designs and Earthbound Clothing, and shoes from Pie Footwear. For around the home I also have a few silk goodies, just for fun. The thought of a worm making a duvet cover and curtains tickles me no end.

The dude arrives with my box of farm fresh vegetables just as I'm single-handedly carrying a carefully balanced futon into the

Djinn

greige painted house.

"Can I help you?" He puts the box down next to the front door.

"Thanks," I nod.

Like engineers building a titanium house of cards, we maneuver, shuffle, twist and balance, to get the frame up the stairs, with the mandatory huffing and puffing during exertion.

Positioning it in the master bedroom, I get a look at the shaggy haired, but neat, dude.

"Moving in?" he asks.

"Yup."

"Cool spot, congratulations."

"Thanks." It is cool, I dig it.

"No missus?" he pries.

"Not yet," we share a smile before descending the stairs. I give him his money and a tip, wiping clinging hair off my forehead.

Diverting to the kitchen, I grab a fruit juice before going to sit in the empty lounge, imagining how it will look when I'm done. I think a leather lounge suite would look cool, with a few hemp rugs chucked here and there. No mirrors this time, and I'm not sure I'm that keen on art.

No missus, not yet. I wonder how Cindy's doing?

Checking my phone again, I have no missed calls from Cindy or Heather.

I'll never figure out the opposite sex.

The one thing I can't live without is music. I'm going to have to go back and get my CD's and player. I wonder if it will work if I pack them in rock salt?

Nodding confirmation to myself, I grab the box from the vegetables, it's big enough to pack both in, heading for the tropical fish store because I know they sell non-iodized rock salt.

Poppet

Getting back to Para-Dice, I notice her the second I pull up. Taking a deep breath, I get out with my box and salt, heading for the shocking-white blond sitting in front of my door.

"What are you doing here?" I ask, walking past her and opening the door.

"I made you these," she says, offering a basket covered with a gingham cloth.

"This reminds me of a fairy tale. Are those poisoned?"

"You don't even know what they are," she scowls.

Lifting the cloth, the scent of chocolate and nuts wrapped up in sticky freshly baked dark sugar make my mouth water.

"You eat one first." I give her a grin so she knows I'm kidding as I move to the lounge to pack my CD's.

"Are you moving?"

"You're very observant," I say sarcastically, pouring salt into cardboard and unplugging the player.

"Where to?"

"Happy Valley."

"Isn't that a bit sudden?" she says.

Pausing, eyeing the basket again and then her with new pink streaks in her hair, I state, "I can't live here."

"And it's all my fault."

I nod, looking back at my task, "Pretty much." Piling CD's in, I attempt to ignore her.

"I went for my Burlesque lesson this morning."

"Cool," I say, still not looking up.

"I thought the pole dancing would be fun."

"Uh huh."

"So I took a pole dancing lesson too. You're not very subtle with your gifts."

"I was naïve and stupid," I mumble. I look up and give her

Djinn

my stone stare. She takes a cookie and offers me one. After she bites into hers, chewing and swallowing, I give in to temptation, taking one and shoving it all in my mouth. I'm starving.

"I want to make it up to you."

I raise an eyebrow in answer, chewing.

"Come out for a drink with me tonight. I'll take you to Calypso's Crypt."

Swallowing, "What time?"

"Eight?"

I nod, "If I'm there, I'm there, if I'm not, you can leave at nine knowing I couldn't make it."

Her mouth twists unhappily and I look down, packing in more CD's.

"I hope to see you there."

I keep looking down when she stands and walks over to me, placing a kiss on my nape before shuffling out.

I don't look up until I hear her car leave.

Sitting back, I pull the basket closer and tuck in, realizing Happy Valley is east of here.

Moving to eagle indeed.

The ceiling vibrates. Staring up at it, I wonder if this is a permanent fixture.

BANG.

"Oh, fuck off. Save your scare tactics for someone who gives a shit."

BANG.

Considering how the house tried to eat me before, I grab the basket and box, getting out of the front door without incident.

Leaving without looking back, I will never return to this house, and if it doesn't sell, I'll burn it to the ground.

Poppet

 **Chapter 22**

Cindy:

I wait for him at the bar, quietly sipping a Pink Bitch. It's fairly close to a strawberry daiquiri, but I dig the name.

Wearing a watch for a change, I keep a close eye on the time. At nine, I'm pissed off.

"Two more Pink Bitches please," I tell the bartender.

He delivers them, not giving me a second glance.

I must be losing my touch.

Swiveling in my chair, I look at the minions clinging to their sulphuric shadows. Downing bitch one, I chase it down with bitch two.

Getting up, I swagger in cowgirl boots to the dance floor doing the saloon strut. Time to party, single girl style. Fuck him.

Looking up, I have ten faces staring at me.

"And?"

I stare back at the ugly man who looks like he hooks nipples and tongues for a living, even his head is tattooed.

"And what?" I say, shocked.

A smelly man in a stained shirt leans forward in his chair, "What happened next?"

Who the hell are these people and why are they all staring at me? "I'm sorry ... what?"

"You can't stop there," the man with the halitosis aftershave

Djinn

chastises.

Leaning back for air, I ask, trying to hide confusion, "What was I saying?"

"You were telling us about the time you were hiding in the Majlis al-Jinn cave in Oman."

I've never been to any such place. This is totally intimidating.

Faking it and needing to escape, I mumble, "Sorry guys, pee break. I've gone blank."

I'm oddly relaxed, as if I've just woken up, experiencing the lethargy of early morning waking as I sift between the crowds to the bricked entrance to the toilets.

Maybe I was sleep talking?

In the ladies, I check my reflection.

Still looking hot.

But now I'm worried and more than a little afraid. Those goons out there are all going to want to corner me and hear the rest of a story I don't know. I don't even know how I got there, who they are, or why I'd come up with such a lie to entertain a crowd of creeps.

Talk about looking desperate. What must they think of me? What kind of girl is that stupid? I'm a lot of things, but I'm not stupid.

It's what? Looking at my watch, twelve-thirty, time to go home. Checking I have my phone and money in my pockets, I fish out the keys and lace them through my fingers like a knuckle duster, getting ready to slip unnoticed past the group hijacked from an L L Bean catalogue meets horror world.

Turning survival instinct up to full volume, I check beyond the door and flit rapidly behind a large crowd of people my age, effectively blocking the strange losers view of me. They're drinking and speaking loudly about me, thoroughly impressed. None of their discussion rings a bell.

Weird.

Poppet

Sneaking behind more big strangers, using them as camouflage, I duck out into the night and flee for my car. Diving in, it takes me minutes to get my hands to stop trembling long enough to get the key into the ignition.

Sasha:

Following the blond with the marshmallow pink streaks in her hair, I don't know what to think.

She completely ignores me when I arrive, giving me a blank stare as if she doesn't know me from a stranger. No recognition at all. And then proceeds to give me the cold shoulder for hours.

Observing her all night while she dances with the burly side of burlesque, then drinks shot after shot with them, telling tall tales and having them riveted to her every word, the group periodically blast the place with raucous laughter.

Staying behind her, playing darts with Jerry, we share another exchange of shock.

"She's not shy, is she?" he says.

"No. I wonder why she bothered inviting me, just so she can ignore me and point out how easy it is to pick up weirdoes."

"She's a whack job, Sash. Let's leave, this is getting boring."

That's when she got up and went to the ladies, leaving immediately after.

"Let's go."

"You go, I'm going home."

"But we're in my car," I point out to him.

"Fuck. Here we go."

"If I have a witness, at least I will know I'm not crazy."

"Fine," he throws the last dart directly into the bull's eye.

Leaving my drink, I shadow Cindy.

Djinn

We tail her back to her place. A huge part of me is relieved she didn't adopt one of those pirates to replace me on the left side of her bed.

Sitting in the car, risking a smoke, we wait for her lights to come on. They don't.

After fifteen minutes, a nagging worry which increases with every minute gets the better of me, "I just want to go up and make sure she's okay."

"Sure."

"You wait outside the door."

"What for?"

"I just have a bad feeling I'll need the back up."

"Why can't you find a normal chick to date?"

"She was normal."

"That girl hasn't ever been normal."

I give him a glare as I open the car door.

"Is she that good?"

Meeting his gaze over the top of the CR-Z, I confess, "Yes."

Taking the stairs two at a time, I get to her door and knock softly. It swings open on the knock.

Perspiration prickles like splinters as I nudge the door open wider.

"Cindy?"

Pulling Jerry inside with me, I flick the light on.

"Cindy, are you here?"

Soft wailing stutters across the lounge.

"Bedroom?" I ask Jerry.

"What if she's not decent?"

"We'll worry about that when we get there."

He nods, and together we sneak across the open plan lounge and kitchen area to the bedrooms.

Flicking the passage light on, we pause and listen, heads tilted for better hearing while staring around, even checking the ceiling.

Poppet

It's louder, the sound of a wounded animal caught in a jaw trap. Forgetting fear, I know something's wrong and she needs me.

"Cindy!"

Shoving doors open, switching on lights, she's not in the study, or her bedroom. That leaves only the bathroom.

Snapping on the light, I halt, staring at the running blood leaking out of the shower.

Jerry bumps into me and I look away just long enough to share an 'oh shit' exchange with him, turning back, I put my hand against the bathroom door.

"Cindy? Honey?"

The door slams, smashing my fingers in the frame.

"Fuck!"

Jerry takes over, pulling the handle down and shoving his shoulder into the door.

I start banging on the door with my free hand, "Cindy! Open the door!"

The thumping of Jerry's shoulder is overpowered by high pitched screaming coming from inside the bathroom. Every reverberation of the door sends volts of pain into my arm; if fingers could scream, mine have just screamed themselves mute. My temples are pounding along with my desperate knocking.

"Open the damn door!" I yell at her.

Demented bitch.

Ducking, swallowing the agony of crunched fingers, I watch my sparring partner kick the door until it splinters, ramming into it a last time to force it to give.

Opening it from the inside, he finally releases my hand from the crude torture.

"It wasn't locked."

Anxiety returns, holding my wounded hand, I lunge into the bathroom to see her cowering in the shower; four empty light bulb boxes litter the floor around her.

Djinn

Uncovering her head with arms, she opens her mouth wide and wails at me.

"Jesus!"

Immediately my body reacts with shaking. I tilt her head with trembling fingers, staring in horror at the thin glass imbedded in her tongue, preventing her from closing her mouth without impaling the palate.

"Eaaaaaauh!"

Tears are pouring from her eyes, they're unfocused.

I yell at Jerry, "Call 911!" I can't wait, fighting my jeans to get to my phone, dialing the number while softly holding her knee, "Hang on babes."

I can't touch her, she even has glass in her arms.

"Nine one one, what's your emergency?"

It's in stereo as Jerry's speaker phone mirrors mine.

Hanging up, I let him take over, while I start fishing shards off the floor like a child collecting seashells, "Help's on its way. Hang in there baby."

It's hard to look at her, her blood is so raspberry red, streaming out of her mouth, making her gargle and choke, smearing war paint down her chin and into her bra.

Waiting in a hard plastic chair in the hospital, my hand bandaged, I'm grateful I have Jerry to drive us.

"Mister Lewis? You can see her now."

Looking up at the nurse, I nod, straightening my stiff knees and pushing myself upright. I nudge my head for Jerry to follow, and make my way behind the voluptuous woman in white.

Cindy lies still on a bed, looking like a changeling child. I forget how little she is because her personality is so much larger than life, the bed swallows her like a pill on a mammoth's tongue.

Poppet

She's covered in plasters up and down her arms.

Sounding like a Mongol child, she stares empty eyes at me, "Why?"

"Why what?"

"Why do tha' tho me?"

"Me? Fuck Cindy! We had to break down the bathroom door to get to you. You were like that when we found you."

She shakes her head slowly from side to side across the pillow, silent tears continuously rippling her cheeks, "No. I woke up in the shower and you were over me holding the boxes."

Despairing, I look at Jerry, still standing at the foot of her bed, "She needs a shrink Sasha. This woman is more schizo than a kaleidoscope."

The nurse overhears, facing us, "The police have been notified."

"I swear to God that we found her like this. She did this to herself."

"After slamming your hand in the door," Jerry points out in a righteous tone.

Yet pure blue eyes don't waver from my face, heartbroken, her hand snakes across the bed on a thin arm, snaring my fingers.

"Ith's okay. I forgive you. You were mad ath me."

Snatching my hand out of her grasp, I turn and leave the room, surrendering to a long night ahead where I'm the accused. Now I'm really glad I have a witness.

Djinn

 **Chapter 23**

Sasha:

We haven't slept. The cops have inspected the door and finally believe our side of the story. After dropping him off at home, I have a mission on my mind.

Taking out my phone, I call Heather Black. She doesn't even say hello.

"Sasha! Are you okay? Why didn't you return my calls?"

"Wait. What calls?"

"I need you to be my character witness. I tried calling you for days," she says.

"There were no messages on my phone."

"Abraxas, it has to be."

A voice taunts in the back of my mind, 'or Cindy'.

"Are you okay? Where are you?"

"I posted bail. I'm at home. But I can't leave until my hearing."

"Where are you? I need to see you," I say.

After giving me the address, her voice is thick with worry, "Drive carefully Sasha. This isn't over yet."

"See you in thirty. Do you need me to pick up anything on my way?"

"No. Just get here in one piece," she says.

Nodding, I start the engine and engage first gear, "I will. See you soon."

Putting the phone in the hands free cradle, I check the mirrors and make my way back over the river.

Loaded with guilt, I park in front of a stereotypical suburban home with a lawn surrounded with gorgeous flowers.

Stealing my resolve, I walk up the white path to her front door. It opens before I can knock.

"Come in, come in."

Freshly brewed coffee makes my mouth water as the flame-haired Irish beauty takes me to her sitting room.

"I'm so sorry about Graham."

She waves me into a chair and starts pouring coffee, "We knew what we were getting into. He's with God now. We accept the afterlife and don't fear going there." She hands me a cup, "Cheesecake?"

I haven't had breakfast and it's hitting me hard staring at the perfect delicacy between us on the coffee table.

"Please."

As if making idle chit-chat, she starts talking, "Did you get rid of the sign?"

"Yes, and all the stock."

"How?"

"A bonfire."

"Good." Heather stares at me, "In the apocryphal Testament of Solomon it explains how Solomon enslaved demons to help him build the temple. And I've just discovered that the word Jinn means hidden. It's the word for the garden of Paradise –"

"Paradise? Like my Para-Dice?"

"Yes."

"Shit."

"It's also the word for mad."

"But I thought a genie derived from the word genius, which is a guardian spirit."

Djinn

"Like Demon once meant guiding spirit. So which angels fell Sasha?"

"What are you saying?"

"I'm saying they are described as smokeless fire. Like angels that shine bright, can smite, they shine like the sun, even the bible says so, but they do not have smoke with that heat. They're one and the same. What we call demons are fallen angels, and we know this about Abraxas."

"But?"

"The good news is that according to some sources, on judgement day the Jinn will also get judged and either sentenced to paradise or hell."

"That's not going to help me right now."

"Why? What happened?"

"Cindy is behaving really strangely."

"Are you two still an item?"

"I'm not sure." I give her a half hearted smile and slice into my cheesecake with the fork.

"I think she's been possessed, Sasha."

Speaking around a mouthful, I ask,"How?"

"When I was taken over by him, that's what you said happened to her. She has no resistance, no faith, no God. She has no spiritual defense against that."

"So what do I do?"

"Kill that book dead. The longer you wait the worse it's going to get."

I nod, "She's in hospital. I could probably get it now without her knowing."

"Do it. Don't hesitate. Why's she in hospital?"

It takes the next hour to fill her in on everything we've been through over the last week. I have her permission to call her no matter what the hour, and to be at her hearing as a character witness in nine weeks. And she's going to do further digging into how to expel Abraxas permanently. Giving her a hug, feeling less responsible for Graham's death, I head back to Cindy's to find that book and 'kill it dead'.

Except, when I open Cindy's front door, she's sitting in the lounge as if nothing happened, reading it.

"You're home."

"Yes. No thanks to you."

"You're sounding much better."

"The swelling's gone down."

Moving across, I sit opposite her, "Are you okay?"

"I guess."

The silence is strained.

"Maybe I should go?" I say.

"So you're not going to apologise either?"

"I have a witness, or does your amnesia automatically rule out being cleared by the cops and having an eye witness?"

"How handy that he's your best friend."

"What about you? You made me watch you flirt all night long while you ignored my existence."

"What bull! You didn't even show up!"

"I did! I was there from nine to after twelve."

"Crap."

"Did you have a good time at least?" I can't hide the sarcasm.

Ignoring my jibe, she offers me a tin, "Jinn-ger cookie?"

"Ginger? Are you being clever?"

"I got the recipe from this book, they're delicious."

"No thanks, I'll pass."

She gets up and drops the book in my lap, "That's what you're here for, isn't it?"

I choose silence, closing my grip around the spine, wondering if I can make a run for it without all hell clamping down on me.

"You smell like perfume!"

Leaning back she snatches the book and points at the door,

Djinn

"Get out."

"No."

"Whose is it?"

"I visited a friend."

"I know that smell. So the cougar lured you back into her lair, did she? And?"

"Stop being so jealous, I went to her over you, and to offer my condolences for Graham's passing."

"Wow, I bet you'd even pass a lie detector test you have yourself so perfectly convinced."

Annoyed, I stand, choosing to leave before this gets any uglier.

"Take care of yourself."

I'm out the door and halfway down the steps before I hear a muffled response. I have to get away from her, she's spiteful and cruel in this mood.

Getting into the Honda, I look up at the face twisted into a murderous smile. She waves, then flips me the bird.

Looking away, I turn the key, and nothing happens.

Smacking the wheel, I pick up my phone again. "Shit."

Dialing the roadside assistance number, I see her still in the window, smiling at me with triumph.

Poppet

 **Chapter 24**

Cindy:

Rolling over, I smack the alarm to shut it up. Winter's coming and the bite on the air makes me want to snuggle forever. I hate working. It's slavery. Human slavery pretending to be purpose.

But it's really perdition wearing its church inspired Halloween clothes.

Unhappy, I point a toe and stick it out, snatching it back when the cold air sucks on it like a vampire bat.

I need a coffee maker. One with a timer.

Sighing heavily, I force myself to sit up and pull on my gown.

Nice gown. What happened to my kimono?

Padding over to the window, I open the blinds, staring out at an unfamiliar view.

Where am I? Did I come home with Sasha? Where does he live now? I don't think he gave me the address.

Walking over a thickly woven carpet, I open the bedroom door and stare at a spacious hallway.

How loaded is he really? He must have inherited an oil rig when his dad died.

Check it out.

Looking everywhere, all I can find in this whole huge house aside from lots of furniture, is Djinn, on an Ottoman in the sitting room.

Djinn

Finally discovering the kitchen, I make coffee.

Checking the garage while sipping it, I see the Honda parked in the double garage on shiny epoxy.

Fancy.

Maybe he went for a run?

Or, maybe he took my car to go somewhere?

Despite the overwhelming desire to investigate and snoop, I go back up to the bedroom, hoping I have clothes here for work.

Looking in every closet, all I can find are my clothes. And someone else's, who's my size and female.

I wish I had more time to find out what's going on.

Searching the bed and bedside tables, I finally locate my phone. Sitting down, slugging back the last of my coffee, I phone him. It bleeps rudely in my ear, telling me the subscriber I have dialed does not exist.

It will have to wait.

Going back to the closet, I select clothes, yanking them on, then move to the bathroom.

Wow! This is some pad. Marble everything, with thick vanilla scented towels next to the bath and shower. My whole apartment could fit in here.

I'm relieved to discover a pink toothbrush with familiar looking cosmetics. Washing my face, brushing my teeth, I then set about putting on the work mask.

Finishing up, I brush my short hair with two pink streaks on the right side.

Skipping back down carpeted stairs, I can't find a purse. But I do find a wad of money and car keys under the hall mirror on a table, as if left there for me.

How thoughtful is he?

But how weird that I can't phone him.

Taking his car keys, I go to the garage and get into the white Honda CR-Z.

Poppet

I'm moving up in the world, obviously.

Driving down the road, I keep driving, taking turns, until I find something familiar. Recognizing McDonald's, I follow the route to work, checking the gas tank.

I wish I could remember what happened last night.

Parking in my usual space, I take the walk to the library. Keeping a watchful eye for nasty apparitions, I go to the administration section, to my office.

Walking in, I see the matron still wearing her pilgrim inspired clothes, "Morning Judy."

She pushes her spectacles up and stares at me with her mouth hanging open. Too much inbreeding there, and it shows.

Rounding the corner, there's a student-looking brunette at my desk.

"Can I help you?" I ask her in a tone interjected with 'get the fuck off my chair you snoop'.

"I'm sorry?" she says.

"You'd better be, that's my desk."

She laughs, looking at Judy who's now behind me.

"Are you lost?" she says, pushing away from my computer, "The main library is downstairs, I think you may have taken a wrong turn."

"I work here, you stupid moron," I snap.

Judy's frail voice squeaks behind me, "No, you don't."

Twisting around to look at her, "What do you mean? Shees! I was only off for a few days and you've already replaced me?"

"You quit, remember?"

"Why would I quit?" I demand.

She shakes her head, "Very funny, Cindy. Now, what are you really doing here?"

"This is insane. Did you smoke crystal meth last night or

Djinn

what? This is my desk and I want it back."

She assumes a haughty expression, looking down her nose at me while peering through inch thick spectacles, "You always were a good liar."

"Why? What the hell is going on?"

"You told us you won the lottery, and you weren't very nice about leaving."

"I'm not nice. But if I'd won the lottery I think I would know about it, don't you?"

"You were even in the paper. You said a red stone gave you good luck."

The Urim dice.

What the heck?

"When did this happen?" I ask.

She looks annoyed, making dilly circling motions against her temple to the idiot in my chair, like I'm a nut case.

"Weeks ago. You're too good for the likes of us now."

Flustered, my cheeks are burning, while the two of them stare at me like I've lost my mind. They're looking insistent and like they mean every word. I don't think Judy has the DNA to pull off a joke, so she's not kidding with me. I'm going to have to fake my way out of this.

"Oh. Right. How silly of me. I think I'm having a throwback day."

"Throwing you back is what we'd love to do with you. I suggest you leave before I call security," the fat old coffin dodger says to me.

"Bitch," I grumble, as I walk rapidly back past her and into the ancient hallway to the stairs.

I wish I knew what the hell is going on.

Is this someone's idea of a joke? If it is, it isn't bloody funny.

Poppet

Chapter 25

Sasha:

God that's heavy. Trying to turn over to alleviate the weight on my chest, it's impossible.

Flopping back, my head is throbbing like I have a hangover.

Trying again, I manage to reach the lamp and switch it on.

"God!" I wheeze.

Cindy has a way of doing maniacal things that scare the shit out of me.

"What are you doing? Get off," I warn her.

Staring up into green eyes, it dawns on me that she's wearing her homicidal smile again.

"Cut the crap, Cin. Move."

But she doesn't, she just keeps sitting on my chest, glaring at me, unblinking.

Trying to edge up with her on me, my body's like hefting a dead vagrant off a bench.

Why am I so tired?

"Please? Come on," I wheedle sweetly.

Shuddering, I hinge upright reflexively when I notice her elbows and wrists are both pointing and bending the wrong way.

"Jesus!"

Shoving at her, repelling her off me, I rely heavily on my instinctive combat training to dart to the other side of the room,

Djinn

now fully awake.

"Stop it." Snapping my fingers at her, "I don't like you, I want to speak to Cindy."

She shrieks before running at me like a silver-back gorilla at full charge.

This version of Cindy is quick and fast and I know I won't get past her to the door.

A confrontation it's going to be.

She halts just out of arm's reach.

"This is getting tiring. Back off," I tell her sternly.

Her chin notches up with supernatural jolts, a garbled oath being muttered in a strange tongue flicks its hate at me.

Ready to block, I feign a lunge.

She takes three rapid steps back, both knees bending the wrong way.

Oh fuuuhk.

"I know you're in there, Cindy. Fight back. Please fight back."

From behind her back, she expertly hurls a dagger at me, the blade clasped between two fingers. She must have been practicing her pegging technique. Pirouetting instinctively to miss it, I snatch her wrist and repel her at the wall beyond me, running for the door.

The lamp cord does the Hokey Pokey, tripping me up. Falling, my breath is shunted out of me when she dives onto my spine with another vicious scream.

Snagging my hair, she starts pulling at it, hissing her arsenic. "No wonder your parents died. They killed themselves to get away from you. I'm going to kill myself to get away from you too. I hate you! Precocious maggot."

Her strength under the influence is alarming and I've no choice but to be a victim, prone like this with her on my shoulders and a knee firmly in my coccyx, where I can't grab anything or see what she's going to do, when she grips my hair, forcing my head back and smashing my face into the floor. "Hate you! Shit satchel!"

Tasting blood, a part of my soul fractures with the incessant abuse. I take a deep breath, knowing getting angry is exactly what it wants me to do.

Rolling, heaving, trying to unbalance her, I buck, getting a knee under me and pushing.

"You're such a deceitful bastard. Was she good? What does a fifty year old pussy feel like? Do you have mommy issues? Trying to climb back into the womb?" My elbow caves when the blade connects with my tricep, "Hate you!"

"Fuck! Cindy, stop it!"

"Stop it Cindy. The truth hurts Cindy. I want a mommy Cindy. One who's old and flabby and smells like Jezebel."

Twisting with every ounce of survival instinct I wrestle her for the knife, finally flipping us. I hold her down with my weight.

She unleashes another anguished howl, in my ear for good measure.

"Fuck off, Abraxas," I snarl while struggling.

"What are you doing in my house, whore? Why come back to me after lathering yourself in her stink?"

"Oh, you've stocked up on your Satanite all right." Pouncing off her, I position myself between her and the door. "Get original demon, or piss off out of that meat suit."

"Hahahaaaaaaa! **Pathetic**. You just can't take it like a man. You want to fuck like one, but refuse to own the rest of your actions."

"I'm not doing this with you," I state flatly.

"I've lost count of how many times you've done it with me. Losing your mind, Sasha?"

Pissed off, I leap for the door, slamming it closed behind me and locking it.

Djinn

THUMP.

Bang bang.

"Sashaaaaa."

It's the sing song voice.

"I'm sleeping in the other room. I'll let you out in the morning," I say through the door.

"Oh come on baby, you know I was just teasing you."

"Goodnight Cindy."

THUMP.

"Fuck you! Just fuck off you lying, cheating, fucking bastard!"

BANG.

Still shaking, I go to the guest bathroom to survey the damage. Inspecting my teeth coated in haemoglobin and the blood trickling a ticklish path to my lips from my nose, I wonder if I'm going to have two black eyes tomorrow.

She has issues, and I can't fix them.

Gripping the basin, tight, so my hands don't tremble, I attempt to breathe the knot out of my solar plexus, employing the zen techniques I learned at Buddhist camp. Unable to stare at my own blood on the white porcelain any longer, I rinse the mess off with ice cold water.

Moving to extract tissues to dab at my nose until the bleeding stops and sinking down onto the edge of the bath, I give in and have a quiet cry.

On my way to the second bedroom, I can hear glass smashing and breaking along with the worst cussing I've ever heard from a woman. Taking a left turn, I take a detour to the bourbon. I need a drink and a smoke, stat. I'm losing my tolerance. I know I cursed her by giving her a blood bond with the fucking thing, but this is out of control.

Poppet

I finally go to bed at three-forty. Struggling for sleep, I consider going home.

A blood fissioning scream rips through the house.

Jesus!

Putting the light back on, my strength deserts me with automatic dread.

"Cindy?!" I call out, into the hall from the safety of my bed.

Silence.

Forcing wobbly legs to walk into the hallway, switching on all the lights, I inch toward her door.

"Cin?"

A deafening scream that sounds like she's being slaughtered comes from the other side of the door.

"Help."

Sobbing.

"Please, oh God. **Someone help me! Goooood!**"

Bloody hell! The neighbors must think I'm beating the shit out of her.

"Cindy?"

"Sasha!"

Another scream that sends my scalp scrambling behind my ears propels me into action.

Unlocking her door, I fling it wide open.

"Oh god." I swallow.

A bloodied hand trembles at me with the fingers all dislocated, reaching for me. Her eyes are blue again, a sure sign it's her.

"Cindy?"

"Help ..."

"What happened?" Kneeling next to her, I try to assimilate the damage through all the blood.

Leaning over her, inspecting her wounds, searing pain keels me over.

Djinn

"Fuck you, you bastard!"

Rolling back, I feel the hilt of the knife in my back. Grunting, I crawl to the phone, managing to dial 911 with slippery fingers coated in blood gloves when she shoots off the floor and body slams into the ceiling, screaming sheer murder until she passes out, hanging limply like a body mobile wanting to be a ceiling fan.

Her heels thudding into the ceiling board like a boat moored too close to the jetty is the last straw. Fighting oblivion, I struggle to remain conscious, gripping a phone in each hand, the landline in my right hand answers first.

"Nine one one, what is your emergency?"

"My girlfriend just stabbed me."

Poppet

Chapter 26

Sasha:

I don't know where I found the sanity but I managed to record her with my phone before the cops arrived. Making me sound less insane and far more credible. It's also the evidence we need to get Heather off the hook.

I'm tired of questions, I'm tired of pain, I'm just tired.

"You can go," the cute nurse says to me, implying I should get off the examination table as I'm taped up and have a prescription for pain killers.

She smiles at me, wiggling a pert bottom as she silently walks out of the room with purpose.

I meet Jerry's worried frown with a numb sensation which refuses to move my facial features. Who needs Botox when you can achieve the same thing with sleep deprivation.

"I can't do this any more, Jer."

"I don't know how you lasted as long as you did," he says.

"Did you see my phone?"

"Yup. I'm never eating her food again. What does she put in it, baby's blood and wedding rings from the people whose fingers she's chopped off?"

"It's the book."

"No way. You have to have the potential to be a bad person to turn into one. Stop making excuses for her," he snaps.

Djinn

"Can I see her before being discharged?"

"Go ahead, but I'm not coming with you," he says.

"I wish you would."

"It's your shit, you deal with it."

I nod, moving carefully. I've been stitched up, she didn't hit anything major, there's really nothing much I can do but take it easy while I heal.

"Are you going to help me get my shirt on, or are you just going to stand there looking judgmental?" I ask him.

He shakes his head, a smile finally squeezing onto his severe face.

It's with trepidation that I stand on the threshold of her room. She's been given a private one out of safety concerns for the other patients.

Walking slowly to the end of the bed, I watch her sleeping, looking fragile and angelic simultaneously.

Despite his objections, Jerry follows me in, pacing like a burglar casing the joint.

The heart monitor beeps regularly, ticking like the countdown to lift off. When she wakes fireworks are going to look tame. She's pyroCind, not pyroclast.

Her fingers are back to normal, along with her joints. I wonder if the doctors fixed that or if they automatically reverse to normal positioning once the evil subsides long enough to give her control.

Two eyes open and watch me. They're blue.

"Hey," I whisper, moving so she can view me with ease.

"What do you want? Come back to finish the job?"

She sounds groggy, as if she was given tranquilizers which are wearing off.

Poppet

"Finish the job? You literally stuck a knife in my back," I say.

"All I remember is waking up in an ambulance, smashed into little pieces by the man I love."

She has a way of extruding guilt so it wraps around you like a garroting piano wire.

"I didn't do this to you."

"I wish I believed you. Show me your knuckles, I bet my blood is still on them," she says hoarsely.

Her eyes sparkle with unshed tears, but her voice cracks and the emotional fissure between us deepens further.

"I have proof," I state.

"I don't want this hurt, Sasha. My heart's far more broken than my body. You seem like such a gentle soul, but you put me through so much trauma I black it out. I can't cope with it psychologically."

Jerry has an expression that could boil her alive, striding around the bed and shoving my phone's screen in her face. "This is the truth. You're the monster here, not him."

Trying to stop this, I'm not sure she's strong enough to deal with the truth without going into shock, "Jer, leave it." Reaching for my camera, I try to shove it down, away from her.

The last thing we need is to resurrect the beast inside her for a full blown demonic retaliation in a hospital, because we antagonized it when it was dormant. I don't know what it is that makes her flip, but I'm not risking seeing it again. Although, at least we're in the right place for resuscitation.

He shoulders me away, "This bullshit ends now, Sasha. I'm sick of listening to this madwoman accuse you to her friends and the authorities. She's done so much damage she can't even begin to undo what she's done to you. You're collecting so many scars from her attacks you look like Frankenstein made you."

The heart monitor goes berserk, her pulse escalating like the drumming in the inipi, and a nurse bursts in.

Djinn

"Visiting time is over. Please leave."

Cindy's crying and it chisels off another piece of my soul to see her so alone and unstable. She must surely be afraid if she doesn't remember.

This reminds me. She said her dad had dementia. Maybe mental illness runs in the family?

Letting Jerry lead me away, I grumble so no one will overhear, "Forcing her to accept the truth isn't going to help. She must be out of her mind afraid if she has amnesia."

"Amnesia fucking bullshit. Isn't that what murderers say to get out of the guilty plea? Ha!"

For safety's sake, I've got another phone as a back up, keeping it in the car in case she smashes my normal one in a rage. It's got a charger in the car under the driver's seat for emergencies which can plug into the lighter.

Using this one, I call Heather while Jerry drives me back home.

"Hello Mrs Black, how are you doing?"–

"Not so good, we've had another incident." –

"I'm on my way home now, but I just wanted to let you know I have recorded proof of Cindy floating on the ceiling and jerking around, I'll be giving it to your lawyer as soon as I can drive." –

"I will, you too. – Bye."

"Why'd you phone her with that phone?"

Staring determinedly at the road in front of us, I say, "I have my suspicions that someone goes through my phone deleting calls and messages from other women."

"Oh yeah, that reminds me, Rachel and Derrick called me when they couldn't get hold of you or Cindy."

"Mmm? How come?"

Poppet

His mouth squiffs into a sardonic squiggle, "I'll let them explain it to you. Do you have her number?"

Thumbing through the menu, I shake my head, "Nope."

He hands me his phone, "It's under Rachel."

Getting home, I lay down on the carpet in the lounge, silently thanking my parents for leaving me wealthy enough to not have to work a day in my life, and for being able to buy whatever I need, whenever I need it.

I wonder if Cindy thinks I'm after the money she won?

Thinking about her snags my heart, and I sit up and take the beer Jerry offers with gratitude.

We clink bottle necks together, while he lights us both a smoke.

"Time to phone Rachel," he instructs, sitting down on the mahogany brown leather three-seater and turning on the widescreen.

Taking a drag, I prop myself up against the sofa and listen to the ringing phone in my ear.

Cindy:

I'm totally lost in this house. I don't know it at all and it's not even my taste. I feel like a visitor in my own home.

And I miss him something awful.

Curling up in the den with Djinn, I open it and stare at an empty page. Paging through it, they're all blank.

"Are you not talking to me now?"

The page remains the same.

"You said you were going to change my luck. I wanted Sasha, where is he?"

I'm not responsible for the things you do when you're drunk.

"But I wasn't—"

Yes you were. I counted those Pink Bitches. How many did

Djinn

you drink?

"Three."

Nine, plus eighteen flaming Sambuca's.

"Oh."

He sounds like a disapproving mother.

"How do I get Sasha back?"

You don't want him back.

"Yes, I do."

You won the lottery. Don't you think you're getting greedy? I've already given you more than most people will ever have.

"I want Sasha. Give him to me!"

I miss my Ouija board, at least it wasn't petulant.

Djinn flies off my lap and hovers in the middle of the room.

Oh crap.

By some unseen force, I'm shoved off my chair and balled into the corner behind it.

"Stop it!"

Straining for all I'm worth against the pressure holding me unnaturally into the wall, Djinn swoops back down, smacking me repeatedly on the head, forcing me to cover my hair with my hands, and it's so sore it's like being whacked on the hands with an anvil.

"Stop it!"

It doesn't stop, thumping me again and again and again, until the room tilts and my vision goes black.

Sasha:

It's been three weeks and I'm relieved to get her call.

"Hey."

"Hey," I say back to her hushed tone.

"Sash, I think I'm going mad."

Poppet

"You have to get rid of that book, babes. It's the source of all your problems."

"I can't," she says.

"Can't, or won't?"

I can hear her crying softly, trying to hide it, "It beats me."

"It beats me why you don't burn it," I laugh.

"No. It hits me. It beats me the way you beat me."

Wait. What?

"I didn't beat you. But say that again. It what?"

"It hits me and bullies me."

"How?" I ask.

If I hadn't seen the things I've seen there's no way I would believe her, but she sounds timid, like she's phoning me from the pantry, hiding in her mansion.

"If I challenge him, the book smacks me something terrible, and unseen forces shove me around and hurt me."

"I'm sorry to hear that." What else can I say? She should have burned it when Heather told us to, but instead she left me to be imprisoned by Haydes inside my own home, *after* I rescued her.

This brings back bad memories.

"I miss you," she whispers.

"I'm sure you do."

"Can ... I mean ... do you think we could get together for old time's sake?"

"I don't know, Cin. You're pretty volatile."

The weeping is louder now and it's tugging my heart.

"I'm sorry I bothered you."

"Don't hang up. Tell me what you're up to these days," I coax.

"Nothing."

"Oh come on, don't be like that."

"I mean it. I never go out, I never do anything. Just call me a recluse. I don't trust myself so I stay home all the time."

"And play music? Or bake? Or read? You must do something

Djinn

with your time," I say.

"I don't know." Her tone reaches an unstable pitch. "I don't remember much, Sasha. I have these holes and miss entire weeks without knowing what the day is or where I've been."

"You need a priest, baby."

"I need you."

Fuck.

"Maybe on the weekend? We'll go out just the two of us?" I suggest.

"Could you rather come to my place?"

"Sure, I suppose." I'm certifiable. I just signed my own death warrant.

"I'll make us dinner," she says, sounding calmer.

"I'll bring Indian take-out instead, like old times."

"I'd love that." The sniffling is smudged with a happier, hopeful, tone.

"Me too."

"Sasha, no matter what, please know, I really do love you."

"Thanks, that means a lot."

"Okay, well, thanks for the chat."

"Take care," I mumble.

"Bye."

I hang up and stare at the phone, wondering if now would be a good time to get a Kevlar vest.

Cindy:

Why's it so dark?

It's so hard and rigid. Shifting, I sit up and look around. It must be the dead of night.

Why don't I ever leave a light on?

Slipping as I stand, I feel my way along the wall, my feet

touching carpet, trailing my hand around the corner, I feel for a light switch and flip it on.

Oh God.

Strength deserts me when I look down.

Where's all this blood from?

Despairing, I slide down the wall, balling into the fetal position and bursting into tears.

My breaking heart is killing me.

I'm so alone.

And mad.

Someone's turned my arms into rulers with blood lines.

Sobbing, the stinging hurts, smearing blood over my clothes, I hug myself, afraid.

"Someone help me!"

"Please ..."

Djinn

 **Chapter 27**

Cindy:

I look so pretty. I know I do. And I'm so apprehensive, I have a bubble of joy and dread doing the jive in my stomach when the doorbell rings.

    He does the best thing. He's not formal, he just wraps me into a hug when I open the door. "Hey babes."

    "God, I missed you," I whisper against him.

    My arm lifts off his shoulder, "What happened to your arm?"

    "I don't know."

    "Are you cutting now too?" he says.

    "I doubt it. I'm a bit on the squeamish side."

    He pulls away to look into my eyes. "You doubt it? You mean you don't know?"

    I shake my head, closing the door, "No. I don't remember."

    "Crikey Cin, you're losing weight."

    "I don't have much of an appetite these days."

    "Well, good thing I brought us Indian food then."

    "Wow, look at you. You're looking great. Nice hair cut."

    He gives me his shag-me-quick grin, taking the bag from the door and heading to the kitchen.

    "Have you been here?" I ask curiously.

    How does he know where the kitchen is?

    He pauses, "You're joking, right?"

Poppet

Crap.

"Of course I am." I laugh to reinforce this, but don't remember him ever being here.

We split the food up, eating, drinking, smoking and laughing. Giggling, I lean on his shoulder when we adjourn to the lounge and curl up on the couch.

This is like old times and I can feel the magic zinging between us. He makes my world normal and safe.

"I think I have to pee."

"Then by all means, don't let me stop you," he says with a hypnotic smile.

Kissing him, I go back the way we came, to go upstairs.

Sasha:

Well this has been pleasant. So far so good.

I wait so long my leg's gone to sleep. Wiping tired eyes, I decide to go looking for her, stomping my foot to get the blood flowing.

"Cindy?"

Taking the cream carpeted steps up to the second floor, I follow the familiar path to her bedroom. The bathroom light is on.

Maybe she passed out?

"Babes?"

Sneaking a peek around the frame, the first thing I notice is she's put the magical corset on.

"You okay, honey?"

Oh for fuck's sake.

"Cindy, put the razor down."

It's like she's not hearing me, sawing into her leg with a rusty blunt razor.

"Cindy."

She moves to the other leg, a glazed expression in her eyes.

Djinn

Moving closer, carefully, I clamp a hand around her wrist, "Cindy, stop."

She pauses, staring at my hand as if trying to make sense of it.

"Come on, let's clean you up."

Even with blood running down her pale legs, something about this svelte babe turns me on.

It could even be the crazy innocence she has despite doing the most insane things. She's like a puppy, completely trusting, standing and letting me lead her to the basins in nothing more than a red corset and a sheer g-string.

Wetting a cloth, I'm hoping there are plasters and salve in this cupboard. Wiping her leg, I'm relieved to see the cuts aren't deep.

"You're going to be okay –"

SMASH.

She slams her head into the bathroom mirror.

"Cindy, stop it."

She doesn't hear me, staring deeply into her own eyes in the shattered reflection, she slams her face into the glass again.

Fuck!

Gripping her shoulders, I tell her in my military tone, "Stop it."

That's when her eyes finally focus on me.

Cindy:

What are you doing!?
No!

I'm smacking him, but I'm not controlling it. *Jesus, I'm going to be sick.*

Sinking my teeth into his arm when he moves to hold my hands, I bite down until I can taste blood and my cheeks hurt.

Poppet

No!
Stop it! Please!
"Cindy!"
I respond with a scream that sounds horrifically insane.
Sasha, I'm so sorry! It's not me! I'm right here. Help me.
What's going on? This is wrong! You can't do this!
STOP IT!

I'm rolled head over heels, hitting my head on the kitchen island. Lunging for the pot on the stove, I grab it and swing it mightily against his head.

How did we get to the kitchen?
Would you fucking stop it!? That's my man. Don't you dare touch him again or I'll kill you! I mean it!

He staggers, wobbling like a drunk before falling against the counter, gripping it with white tense fingers.

The screaming, oh lord, shut up! Stop screeching. I hate you! Stop it right this minute.
Shut up!
What are you doing?
Stop it!
You're hurting him, God damn it!

Crying, sobbing, I'm helpless, watching his face when he looks up at me with confusion and fear.

You're breaking his heart, please, oh Jesus please stop.
I can't look.
I hear the crunch.

My entire body is cold and quaking, but on the outside, something else is calm and using my body to hurt him. I'm incarcerated inside my own body.

This isn't possible. This is a dream. A very, very, bad dream.

Terrified, stuck in the dark but knowing this is me, but it's not me.

Let me out!

Djinn

Waaaaail.
No, sniff, oh no.
NO!

Clawing at him until his arms are red and sticky, his skin under my nails thick and disgusting, I listen to myself laughing.

Leaning back, I light a smoke and sit down to watch him bleed.

You bastard!
Look what you've done!
I love him, and you're killing us.
You're killing his soul!

Opening my eyes, I look at Rachel.

Rachel:

"Do I look ready to have coffee with my ex best friend?" I ask him.

"As ready as you'll ever be. Are you sure you want to go alone?"

"I'm not chancing her making a scene at you in Peet's," I say.

"Rachel, please be careful."

"I will. We have to set this up so Djinn doesn't know what's coming, it's the only way." I reassure Derrick.

"I love you muffin."

"Derrick, stop worrying."

"Is your phone charged?" he says.

"Yes."

"Okay." He folds me into a breath stealing hug before letting me go and opening my car door.

Smiling, giving him a quick kiss, I slip behind the wheel.
She arrives on time, wearing a long sleeved white shirt and black jeans. Her hair is shorter than usual, and she gives me a tired

smile as she slips her slender frame into a chair at the table.

"Hi Cinders. I'm glad you could make it."

"I'm so sorry, I don't even know where to begin apologizing."

"Oh, Sash said you couldn't remember."

"I can't, but he told me what happened."

"Just don't do it again," I tease.

"Do what?"

"Huh?"

"Sorry, what were we talking about?"

"Nothing, shall we order?"

"I'm dying for some real coffee. My machine makes crap coffee."

"How is life now that you're a wealthy woman?"

"I'm not wealthy."

I'm not sure if she's utterly bonkers now, or pulling my leg.

"Cindy, you won a shit load of cash."

"I did? When?"

"Remember the night we went to the Sliding Door and you bought a lottery ticket?"

"Oh yeah. That was fun. I haven't been to Dantés in ages."

"Well life's changed a lot since then."

"Why are we here? Shouldn't we order a round of coffee or something?"

I nod at her being erratic, "What would you like?"

"Cappuccino and chocolate cake."

"I'll go order."

She nods, slumping back in her chair and passing out.

"Crap." Leaning over her, I check that she's breathing.

She sits up abruptly and blinks at me, "You okay?"

"I'm fine, are you okay?"

"Shouldn't we order coffee?"

"I was just going."

"So don't just sit there, go."

Djinn

Giving her my strange scowl, I go to the counter to get our order. Keeping an eye on her, I return with our drinks and cake.

"Oh cool, coffee! Rachel! What are you doing here?"

"Hi Cindy. I saw you over here and thought I'd bring you some cake and coffee."

"I hate chocolate cake, how typical of you."

"You are messing with my sanity right now, Cin."

"Jesus, don't make such a big deal out of it. If it means that much to you I'll eat it."

She yanks the plate off the tray and stabs the cake as if it was my eyeball.

Sitting opposite her, I inhale slowly to keep a grip on my temper.

We sit in silence, sipping and eating. I'm watching her closely and periodically she stares off into space, frozen. Sometimes with the fork hovering between her mouth and the plate, completely unaware that she's doing it.

"Cindy?"

No response.

"Cin," I say a little louder.

Nothing.

Sitting back in my chair, I wait it out. People are now beginning to stare at us like we're odd. Feeling like a freak, I continue sipping my coffee and pretending this is normal.

Twenty minutes later she snaps out of it, "This is great. Just like old times."

"It is, isn't it?" I smile at her.

"So what's new? Getting married yet?"

"Nope. But I was hoping we could have a reunion at your place."

"That would be so cool. When?"

"Maybe this weekend?" I suggest hopefully.

She nods enthusiastically. "Is Sasha going to be there?"

Poppet

"Yes."

Her features soften and tears form in her eyes, "I love him. I really miss him."

"Do you?"

"He was my soul mate. One day he just stopped coming round."

"I'm sure he misses you too," I tell her. There is no way I'm going to be the one to tell her what she did, and how we're planning a bad ass intervention all over her.

"I don't know where all the blood came from."

"What blood?"

"In the war, I was in the trench, and my leg was missing, and I looked down and just saw blood."

What the hell is she talking about?

"Then Tommy started screaming –"

And she slumps in her chair again. This is really bad. Is it Alzheimer's, dementia, possession, or madness? How did Sasha cope with this, at all? That poor man deserves a medal and sainthood.

"Next week's the wedding."

Jarred, I look at her. "Wedding?"

"Yes, Michael's getting married."

"Who's Michael?"

"Belinda, you know Michael's my son. For God's sake you're his godmother."

"How forgetful of me. Are you excited?"

I'm playing this completely by ear.

"I hate the redheaded bitch. She stole him from me, you know?"

"Who?"

"Heather."

"Michael's fiancé?"

"Is she getting married? Already? But Graham only just

Djinn

died."

"Oh, that Heather."

"What are you talking about?"

"I have no idea."

This is becoming so ludicrous I'm tempted to laugh.

"So she and Sasha, aren't, you know?"

"Never did, never will."

"Slut."

"I beg your pardon?"

"You always were the cheer-leading whore."

"Cindy!"

"What?"

"How can you say that?"

"What? All I said was it's cold. Don't freak out." She glares at me and takes a sip of her frothy coffee. "This is crap coffee. It's cold."

"Maybe we should go?"

"But we just got here," she argues.

"I really should go."

"But I miss you, please don't go."

"I'll see you on Saturday with the gang."

"Oh, I'd love that. Will Sasha be there?"

She looks melancholy and sad again.

"I guarantee it."

"How long is the guarantee for? I bought an iron once with a lifetime guarantee, and that was a total lie."

"You're kidding me?"

"The only way to make a decent curry is with habaneros."

I pat her shoulder, "It was nice seeing you, Cindy. Take care."

She grips my hand, her eyes widening dramatically, pleading in a whisper, "Please don't leave me."

"I have to go."

"No. Please! Don't leave me!"

Poppet

Her suddenly loud voice has everyone staring at us.

Awkward, I abruptly sit down again. The panic in her voice unnerves me.

"Rachel?"

"Yes Cindy."

"I was just having dinner with Sasha. How did you get in here?"

"You were?"

"This doesn't make any sense."

She starts trembling violently, her eyes radiating horror, "I was hurting him. But it wasn't me. I couldn't stop it. I was screaming for it to stop. Sasha!"

She drops my hand and stares vacantly out the window. Seeing my only opportunity, I make a mad dash for the door.

What the fucking hell!

Djinn

Chapter 28

Cindy:

Waiting for my vision to focus, I'm dizzy. It's so dark in here. Screwing my eyes up, I stare through the black fog, my hand tight against my temple, waiting for the vertigo to pass.

Where am I?

A terrible dread washes over me like nausea. I'm kneeling on a bed, in a gloomy room, and it smells like puke.

"Who the hell are you!?" I ask the massive man.

Shuddering, I want to put my hand to my mouth with repulsion but am too afraid to do so in case he hits me or something.

I have a really bad gut feeling about this.

The sweat - or oil - on him, wrinkles my nose.

I think I'm going to be sick.

"I've been so wicked. Mistress you must punish me."

I'm looking at a big fat dark man lying under me. Scrambling off him backwards, my heels snag the carpet and I land tush first on the floor.

Hideous purple and gold print damask wallpaper becomes prominent above the bed with its super shiny bed-skirt.

"I ... I ..."

Scrambling, I flip to run, gearing my legs in a runner's position, when I see the man in the chair behind me. Dropping the crop in my hand, I freeze.

He's covered in shadows, the faint light just enough to make out broad shoulders in a black jacket. Taking a step back, I'm caught. I don't know what to do.

How did I get here?

"Who are you and what the hell do you want?" I ask the shadow.

I stare at my arms, buying time to think. Sheer black gloves up to my biceps don't hide the red marks underneath. What am I wearing?

Oh God.

Vertigo jiggles my consciousness again and the room circles in wild arcs. Staggering, I cradle my head, waiting to wake up, for the gyrating madness to stop. "What is this?"

"Cindy? Are you all right, dear?"

Forcing my eyes open, I try to focus on the blurring hulk of the man in the chair standing and advancing toward me.

Crap.

Shrinking back, I stop only when my calves connect with the bed behind me.

Just pretend. Fake it.

"No! I'm not all right."

"Leave us, go and get some air," he says in a kind voice.

Why's he being so nice?

Staring wildly around the purple and black room decorated in sleaze, I'm half crazy out of my mind with fear. Nodding fervently, I scan the large room with plain sections of pure black wall interspersed with royal purple and gold print, looking for the door. Spotting it between two red satin curtains, I trot as fast as my trembling legs will move.

I need to pee so bad.

Bursting into a dimly lit dingy corridor, I hook a left and run in ridiculously high heels.

Djinn

How did I get here? Where am I?

Who were those weirdoes?

Panic messes with my breathing, and I'm gasping, running for ages down corridor after corridor, trying to find a way out.

Where are the god damn doors?!

The peeling paint and stench of urine taints me, adding to my panic.

Locating metal stairs, I take them up, clopping shoes in echoing eeriness with my ascension.

Ploughing into a huge dark suited man at the top, I amble back, almost losing my footing off the narrow platform.

"Smoke break, huh?" He hands me a long woolen trench-coat, "Take your jacket, it's cold out there baby."

"Thanks."

"Always a pleasure for you, Cindy."

I give him a toothpaste advert smile, waiting for the big iron door to open and set me free.

Please – Please...

Don't change your mind, just open that door.

There's a good boy.

Stay calm, keep focused.

He obliges, and I emerge into a night-scape drizzling with rain. My head is pounding like someone's conducting construction inside it.

Pulling the long coat on over tart underwear and sheer hold-up stockings, I rummage frantically through the pockets while sidling along the length of a dilapidated white building. It looks like a disused warehouse, all dark and shrouded, very little light from the street lamp reaches this deep into the loading and parking area.

Looking behind me, checking for predators coming back to kidnap me when they realise I'm making a getaway, I keep searching by feel in the pockets. Finding smokes, money, a phone and a car key, I grab the keys, running to the group of cars parked a good ten meters away.

The parking lot is gravel, my every step sounding loud and boldly announcing where those mobsters can find me. It's also impossible to do this steadily, or fast, in such high heels.

I have to get away.

Now!

Before they come looking for me.

Where's my Mini? Where the hell is my car?

Almost ready to cry, I can't believe I'd bring a car key if I came with someone else. As if I'd ever get into a car with any of those muggers. Anxious, I flay wildly, pressing the remote again and again, listening to a car beeping.

"But, that's Sasha's car."

Who am I to argue, just go - go - go.

Ducking to below car height to hide away, I rush to the Honda, opening the door and quickly getting in. Kicking the shoes off, immediately freezing my feet with cold, I slip the key in with violently shaking hands.

Please start.

Watching the rear view mirror, then darting my focus left and right, I'm looking for an armed guard, or bouncer; a thug lurking to smash the windscreen in and drag me back in there.

I start the engine.

Thank God.

Leaving the lights off, I drive away as sneakily as I can, forcing myself to adopt stealth mode until I hit the smooth tar a few blocks down. Planting my foot down, putting on the safety belt and the lights, I scream rubber through the roads until I locate SE Morrison Street.

Knowing where I am now, I don't even care about tickets, I just want to go home.

It's deserted, like I've arrived here after the rapture. Glancing

Djinn

at the time on the display, it's three twenty-five in the morning.

Still shaking, I take the eerie drive home through slick empty streets lit with jaundiced lights hazed with mist. My right leg vibrates in nervous twitches, making the ride jerky.

"Oh mommy."

My neck is cramping with tension and I feel sick.

All I want is to wash this smell off me.

What did they do to me? Were they filming that? Did they drug me?

They acted like they knew me.

Who the fuck **were** those people!?

God I hope Sasha is home.

I find a spot to park in, close to the entrance. Feeling conspicuous in these horrid clothes, I put the shoes back on and attempt to tiptoe through rivulets and puddles, into the apartment building on 37th Ave.

Almost there.

Running up the stairs, half pulling myself with the railing, I racket up to the second floor. Gripping the coat closed, I take out my keys and slip the key into the lock.

It won't open.

This is **not** happening to me.

Please open.

Please?

Why won't it unlock?

Wait! There's movement inside.

Knocking softly, I call in a hushed voice, "Sasha!"

Shuffle shuffle.

My skin crawls when I hear heavy breathing on the other side of the door.

I knock again in a soft, tap tap. "Sasha?"

Adrenalin pumps gallons through my veins when the chain scrapes back. The handle turns.

Poppet

Instinctively I look behind me, then back at my door as it opens.

"Can I help you?"

An old man in his pajamas holds the door between us, shielding himself as if I'm a lunatic. His shifty eye looks me over, with obvious interest.

Gaah!

Shuddering, I take a step back, slipping and skidding on the polished floor with shoes lubed with water while he drains the mucous from his throat in a blocked garbage disposal slurry.

"I – " What is this? "I um, is Sasha home?"

"No person lives here with that name."

"Who does live here?"

"Me."

"But, is my stuff still in there?"

"Been living here for two months. Only my stuff is in here."

He shuts the door on me, ending the narrative.

He's lying. He's got all my worldly possessions and knows it. Thief!

Ringing the doorbell this time, he grunts from the other side of the door like he's on oxygen therapy and needing it fast, "Go away or I'll call the police."

Slinking back to the stairwell, I sink onto the steps.

I don't know what to do.

Staring through the window at the murky night, my eyes cloud with despair.

I'm lost.

I don't understand what's happening.

Someone has to know.

Panicked, I bolt up and clatter back down the stairs to the car.

Disoriented, I look for my Mini.

Slipping on the walkway, I sit in a muddy puddle, bursting into tears.

Djinn

"How did I get here?"

A shiver sharpens claws down my spine.

I'm going to get arrested. He's going to phone the cops and they're going to take me away and lock me in a nut-house.

Propelling myself off the ground, I fiddle around in my pocket with numb fingers.

Finding keys, I take them out and study them in the faint illumination.

Chancing luck, I depress the button and a white Honda CR-Z's lights flash.

But, that's Sasha's car.

Do I live with him?

Shaking my head, I totter quickly to the vehicle and get in.

So warm in here. Lord, it's cold tonight.

Rubbing my arms, blowing into my hands, I stare worriedly out at the gloomy night.

Shivering again, I put the key in and turn it.

It starts.

Okay, next stop Sasha. Please be there.

I stop the car on the corner of Hawthorne boulevard and SE 37th Avenue and stare at his house.

It's empty.

The windows have no curtains and none of the shutters are closed.

Inhaling deeply to gather courage, I get out the car and walk down the street to his house, up the pathway and to the front door.

Knocking on the door, I move to look in the window.

Dust lies thick on the floor.

Somewhere deep inside a beam creaks and immediately an acid burning fear rises up from my stomach.

Poppet

The desolation and abandoned vibe is thick enough to suffocate on.

My skin crawls in violent shudders, and I back away and run to the car, belatedly noticing the for-sale board on the lawn, blown over.

Safely inside, I grip the wheel and cry. Frenzied fear leaves me weak and shivering.

"Why?"

Sob.

"Why are you doing this to me?"

Leaning back, wiping my eyes and swallowing terror, I force myself to breathe. A random memory enters, and I lean over and open the glove box.

Extracting a box of Marlboro, I roll down the window and shake one out. Lighting it, I am instantly calmer and more in control.

Think Cindy.

Think.

Exhaling a noxious cloud out the open window into the frigid night, I unearth the phone from the woolen coat and stare at it.

Sucking on my cigarette, I skim through the phone book.

Sasha Lewis.

Pressing dial, I wait for the ringing to stop with a twist of anxiety compressing my intestines like a stress ball.

Flicking the butt, knowing there's no one to see me, I burst into tears again at the disconnected tone.

Sniffing, smudging my nose with icy fingers, I lean forward and start the engine again, driving to the public phones, peering through a fogged up window and traversing roads through an abandoned ghost town.

Leaving the car and the window open in case I need a quick getaway, my paranoia of being hunted increases.

My life, someone's stolen my life and left me in limbo.

Djinn

Rushing to the booths, I grab the phone book and rifle through it to Lewis.

Running a quaking finger with chipped nail-polish down the names, there are three Sasha Lewis' listed for Portland.

I don't have any change.

Shit.

Clomping back to the car, I get the cell phone, and shimmy back around the front of the car to the still open phone book.

Plugging in the first number, I wait while it rings.

"Hello?" a groggy voice grinds into my ear.

"I'm sorry to disturb you, I'm looking for Sasha Lewis."

"Speaking."

"Are you the same Sasha Lewis who owned Para-Dice?" I ask.

"Naaaah, think you've got the wrong number."

"I'm so sorry to have woken you." Disconnecting, dread pounds my heart hard enough to make my ears thud. The shudders quaking my body are becoming increasingly violent, and I don't know if it's fear or cold causing them.

Struggling with the phone, I force my jittery fingers to dial the next number.

And the next.

"Hello?"

I know this voice. This is an angel.

"Sasha?"

"Hmm?"

His voice is a balm on fraught nerves and all my terror unleashes, my voice trembles while I sink to the wet ground, holding the phone with both hands. "Sasha, I'm lost."

"Who is this?"

"Cindy."

"Cindy Wolfe?" he says.

"I don't know where I live. I went home and someone else

lives there. Then I went to your house and it's vacant. I don't know where to go." The sobbing overcomes me and I cradle my knees, sitting in the drizzle of a moonless cruel night, rocking myself. "I – I don't know where I live."

"Where are you?" He sounds so confident and calm. Men just take control and make everything fine again.

Visually searching, I say, "Hold on. I have to find a street name."

Forcing myself to kneel and stand, I step back into the road, the heels mock me with their clicking on uneven tar. "I'm at the public phones on Hawthorne ..."

"I know where you are. I'll be there in twenty minutes."

Before I can say thanks, my phone goes dead.

He's my only hope.

Sitting on the curb, I bury my face in my arms and cry.

I'm so scared.

Some time later, a car's engine purrs closer down hollow streets. Trepidation writhes like an alien in my insides as I desperately wipe my eyes and look in every direction, trying to locate it.

I'm parked under a street lamp, easy to spot, but what if it's not him?

What if it's those sex thugs looking for their loot?

Scrambling behind the Honda, I grip the slick paint-work, watching fearfully for car headlights.

It turns and I see them coming toward me like a monster out of the moors.

Shaking so violently with petrified nerves, I hide until the car stops, facing mine, the headlights and engine stay on.

The rain glistens in the light like lethal glitter, slicing the tension with impatient thrumming.

Footsteps.

Djinn

Oh Jesus!

Peeking, I almost pee myself with relief.

"Cindy?"

Forcing myself to stand upright, I forget to close the coat.

He's glorious, wearing a snug white sweatshirt and navy track-pants. His hair is blond and swept away from his face in messy spikes. He's ten times more better looking than I remember him.

"I'm so sorry. I didn't know who else to call."

His eyes sweep over me and he hides his hands inside deep pockets.

"You look like you're into some shady stuff."

My head is shaking left and right, my mouth twisting dramatically, and I force myself to face him, "I came to in a room. I was dressed like this. But I don't know how I got there or who they are." Gripping my hands tight and wringing them to try and force warmth into them with pressure, I blurt, "I want to go home."

"Please take me home," I beg him.

He turns and switches the engine of his car off. The silence swallows us in a hungry void and an echoing loneliness engulfs me.

He's not going to take me home.

Sasha:

Her eyes puddle more than the pavement and a soul chilling desperation coats her voice. I believe her. I believe she has no clue where she lives, and is terrified.

"It's okay, I know where you live."

She takes a wobbly step toward me, "You do?"

She sounds ecstatic. So grateful.

Poppet

"What happened?" I ask.

"I ran. I couldn't find my car but had the key for this one. I probably stole it from someone. I half expect to get arrested. I look like a prostitute and can't remember anything. I drove for my life back to my place, but an old man says he's lived there for two months." She balls a hand over her mouth when a sob escapes, her eyeliner is running red streaks down her face and her entire body trembles like she's in shock. "Then I went to your place – and," she fights for control over her sobbing, "You don't live there."

"I moved."

"When?" she wails softly.

I watch her breath form a vapor cloud in front of her face. She's like a little girl. Despite her appearance she has innocence in her expression, vulnerable and timid. "Months ago."

"And ... us?" she asks.

"We broke up too, awhile ago."

She looks up at the night. "Oh God."

Diving forward, I catch her skull like a bowling ball as she faints, rescuing her from hitting her head.

"Oh Cindy. Never a dull moment."

Djinn

Chapter 29

Sasha:

Facing each other in the rain, we're awkward. We've been everything, but never awkward.

"Did you disconnect your old number?" she asks.

"Yes."

"Why? Did you have to ditch me that desperately?"

I smile at the waif looking so forlorn and drowning in a coat three sizes too big for her. "I left it with Heather's attorney as evidence, and switched over to my back up phone."

"Her!" Her voice and demeanor instantly morph into aggressive nuances.

I'm tired of this bullshit with Heather and Cindy.

"Do you know why you don't like her?" I sneer, stepping closer to stare down into her eyes with as much intimidation as I can muster. Fully aware that provoking her could end in a retaliatory attack.

She tilts her chin up, "Why?"

"Because she has the power to save you, and there's no way your demons want her, or me, near you."

"Rubbish."

"Think about it, Cin. The minute you gave Djinn your blood you wanted to protect that book. At that point the biggest threat was Graham and Heather to its survival. Then when they explained to me how it worked and why we needed divine intervention, you turned on me because then I was perceived as a threat."

"No –"

"Yes. And when it had removed Heather and Graham, you did your damnedest to destroy me, inside and out."

"How? How could I possibly destroy you?"

I push up my sleeves, "Scars you gave me."

"I – what?" She looks shocked. "But I love you. I would never … Would I?"

"You chose a book over me, Cindy. That's how much you love me."

She staggers, falling back against the car and sitting on it, holding her head. "I keep feeling like I'm going to pass out."

"Changing the subject?"

She shakes her head, staring at her feet. "Sasha, this has been the worst night of my life. Please go easy on me, I'm mentally fragile right now."

"Has it ever occurred to you that the dementia your dad had is hereditary? This bullshit with you has been going on for months."

"I … no. Is that what's wrong with me? Am I mad like dad?"

Her expression wrings with appalled realization.

"Possibly. You could also be mad like Jinn. It's another meaning for the word Djinn. Meaning you're under the control of a very bad entity."

She looks up, her face sheened with tears and rain, crying she stutters, "I'm sorry. For everything. I know I hurt you. I know – I have dreams – I hurt you in them. I never wanted to hurt you – it was him, it, not me …" She puts her head in her hands, staring down at her silhouetted legs in car headlights, "I sound crazy."

The fight's gone out of her, her square shoulders hunch and she seems to fold into herself. "I just want to go home," she mumbles at her black shoes.

Djinn

I feel sorry for her, I do.

Moving closer, to offer a hug, she stands, hurt and fear widening her eyes as if I'm about to strike her. Her eyelids are puffed with grief and her irises swim with unshed tears.

While I'm watching, her eyes shift in a rapid succession of flickers, and she collapses again.

Catching her with ease because of close proximity, I lay her gently to the ground, moving sodden white hair off her ashen face.

So beautiful, and so very broken.

I wish I could have saved you before it got to this.

A heavy sigh breaks free from my tension and I observe the make-up and outfit. The powder coating can't disguise the rust. I gave her Djinn. I donated her blood to it. She came to me for help, and I'm duty bound to fix this.

Picking her up out of the rain, I carry her to the car, waiting for her to become conscious again. Holding her cold fingers in mine, I rub my hands together to warm hers between them.

"I'm sorry too."

She can't hear me; it's better this way.

Last night reinforces the decision. That was the old Cindy. The one I loved from afar for years, and the one I went too far to impress. Now I know she's still in there. Which must mean she blacks out when Abraxas takes over, leaving her with no memory of who she's hurt or what she's done.

Seeing her so lost and vulnerable galvanized my guilt. She was ashamed, and delicately fragile in her honesty with me. Risking rejection, she chose to expose her heart. The old Cindy held her emotions to her chest closer than a million dollar poker hand. She must be utterly shattered to be so open, uncaring of the

Poppet

consequences.

And I still feel responsible.

She regained consciousness after about fifteen minutes, drenched from the rain and frozen. Staring at me like a child in a nightmare, so afraid and trembling with terror, clutching my hand and beseeching me to take her home. Seeing her like that, snuffed embers began to burn and I just wanted to make it better.

It was strange and oddly surreal explaining her car and home to her. I had her follow me to her home in the matching Honda to my own, driving at a retired pace while I worried she'd pass out behind the wheel before reaching our destination, and unconsciously crunch into my bumper.

Through the unexpected torrential rain I held the thinner version of her against my side, automatically protective, escorting her inside and to her bedroom. She was disinterested in the house, as if she didn't like what it represented, asking only to be taken to her bathroom and bed.

She told me about the stench bucket she found herself with and it was bile inducing listening to her recollection of the evening.

When she looked at me with beguiling eyes constantly shedding shameful tears, pleading with me to stay with her while she cleaned up, I surrendered. Helping her bathe, the bruises and marks on her body worry me. She said Djinn beat her, and seeing the bruising on her skin, I believe that now too. Although dressed like she was, a large number of those marks could have been delivered in other ways.

Whoever else lives in her head wants to hurt her, and wants to hurt everyone who loves her. There's no self-preservation or pride left there.

To her credit though, I am relieved there are no track marks anywhere on her body, but if this continues, it's only a matter of time.

Djinn

I left her after sun up, tucking her into bed and watching her sleep. Planting a kiss on her chilled skin, knowing better than to take on Djinn alone, I left without looking for it.

It's time to put Rachel's plan into action.

Cindy:

Thud.

Ow.

Rubbing my forehead which I just bashed into something hard, I feel around. I can't see anything. Oh Jesus. I'm in a box. This is definitely a box.

Or a coffin.

"Hello!"

I'm going to run out of oxygen. I read that over eighty percent of people are buried alive and that's why they were once buried with a bell connected to a string so you could ring the bell if you woke up in a coffin six feet under.

Forcing myself to suppress alarm, I feel around for anything that could be attached to a bell.

Shit. Nothing.

Smacking my hand into the lid, "Help! Can anyone hear me?!"

"Help!"

It's so dark. Worming my hands down, I check my pockets in case I have a lighter.

No such luck.

"Hello! Anyone?! **Help!**"

Poppet

Sasha:

"Rachel, it's Sasha."

"Hey! How are you?" she says.

"I'm fairly good."

"To what do I owe the pleasure of this call? You're up to something, I can smell it," she says.

"Cindy called me last night."

"Really? I think she's deliberately lost my number."

"Rachel, it's serious. She was in shock, she thought she still lived in her old apartment. She phoned me because she wanted to go home and didn't know where home was."

"Same shit, different day."

"That's what I thought when she called, but I couldn't leave her out in the middle of the night, lost. I dunno, it was strange, I just had a feeling ..." I say.

"And?"

"It was her. Without the madness. And she's terrified. She needs her friends Raych."

"I don't know, Sash. I don't think I'm ready to be her punching bag again."

"Remember your plan, before she conveniently forgot about us going over?" I ask.

"Yeeeeees?" It's drawn out and doubtful.

"It's time. We have to do this."

"It was a dumb idea," she grumbles.

"No, it's not. Rachel, I feel so responsible, the guilt is the one thing stopping me from just letting the whole past thing go. If I don't try, it's going to be with me for the rest of my life."

"If we do this, I want you to know I'm doing it for you, not for her," says Rachel.

"I understand, and I'm grateful, I really am."

"Shit Sasha. This is going to be awful."

Djinn

"I'm hoping it won't be. We'll be properly prepared this time."

"How?" she demands.

"For starters, we'll have the cops ready and with us in case she starts trying to hack us into pieces, and biting and clawing her way through us. She has the strength of three men when she turns, and we're going to need professionals to deal with that."

"How are the scars?" Her tone is gentle and concerned.

"They're healing." I smile at the sunny lounge as if she is sitting in front of me.

"Okay big guy. We'll do it. When?"

"This afternoon," I say.

"So soon?"

"Yes."

"What time?" she asks.

"Three."

"Are we meeting you there?"

"I think it would be better to arrive together," I nod.

"Me too. Okay."

"Thanks Raych, you're a baby doll, I hope Derrick tells you that often enough."

"Get a new girlfriend stud, hitting on me is gonna get you nowhere."

We laugh and say our good-byes.

Poppet

Chapter 30

Sasha:

Heather is at church, praying through this with Father John, keeping a spiritual vigil. She's been a wealth of archaic information and I spent the rest of my day with her, being educated on pronunciation.

We also have the Shaman saying prayers for us to the Great Spirit in the spirit lodge, drumming the heartbeat of the Earth on his water drum and calling reinforcements.

"Have you got the sea water?" I ask Rachel.

She taps the bucket between her and Derrick.

"If you can't take the book to the ocean, we bring the ocean to the book."

"I've started calling her Mohammed," Derrick teases.

I lose my smile when we pull up in her driveway. Heather's lawyer pulled strings and has as our chaperone a two cop patrol unit who will wait outside in their car, just out of sight, until required. They're already set up with the surveillance.

I'm hoping they won't be needed.

Flexing my jaw in tight tension, my stomach squirms uncomfortably, "I'm leaving the door unlocked. I go in first."

Jerry's grip on the steering wheel is the only sign of his stress, "I'm happy to go in with you."

"We have to catch her by surprise."

Djinn

Opening the car door, I stand, checking my pockets for the handcuffs.

Taking a deep breath, I grab the bouquet of flowers and make my way to her front door. Ringing the doorbell, they all duck out of sight. I know the cops can see everything that's happening by the camera in the button hole of my golf shirt.

Gulping, I face the door, doing my best not to look suspicious.

It opens and I'm face to face with my nemesis.

"Cin, hi." I offer the flowers, "Surprise."

She gives me a stagnant smile, opening the door wider to let me in, stepping into the lion's den I notice her eyes are green. I hope the camera picks that up.

"Come in. How delightful."

My throat closes along with the door, apprehension is so tight through my muscles it's challenging to walk with a relaxed gait.

She gestures to the sitting room, where Djinn parks submissively on the table, closed.

"Have a seat, what can I get you to drink?"

"Nothing yet, thanks."

She nods, walking ahead of me in tight black jeans and tank-top.

Sitting opposite her, I smile, "How are you feeling?"

"Fine. Why?"

"I was a little worried about you after last night."

"I'm fine," she says in curt dismissal. "Why flowers?"

"I haven't ever bought you flowers, it's never too late to start."

I give her my award winning smile, slowly wiping clammy palms on my jeans.

Poppet

Cindy:

It's really dark. Can't see anything. Not even my hand.
    It's warm too, and stuffy. Reaching a hand out, I feel the confining walls. They're like wallpaper.
    Where am I?
    "Hello!"
    "Can anyone hear me?!"
    Nothing.
    It doesn't feel like a coffin. What does a coffin feel like?
    I don't remember anything.
    How the hell did I get here?
    It's too small. I can't move around.
    Oh God, I think I've been buried alive.
    Wait.
    Can you hear that?
    Sounds like voices.
    "Hello!"

Sasha:

    "Are you hinting at us getting together?" she says.
    I shrug in response.
    She's being distant and uncommunicative.
    "I think I will have a drink. Would I be imposing if I asked for coffee?" I say to Cindy.
    "You don't mind if I lace it with solanine, do you? It'll only leave you weak and confused, unless my hand slips and I overdose you, in which case you could go into a nice quiet coma and you won't be bothering me any more."
    "Harvesting your own toxins now?" I say.
    "Green potatoes are so handy, you never know when you might need to accidentally poison someone."

Djinn

My mouth is dry and I get the distinct impression she's not kidding.

She throws her head back, laughing maniacally, "Just teasing. Lighten up."

I smile, pretending to relax back, propping an ankle on the other knee, looking around. "Do you have a cleaner?"

"I clean up the bodies myself. Sacrifices get so messy."

"That's not even funny, Cindy."

"Who says I was joking?" The smile caressing her face is cold and calculating, flat eyes hide the plotting I know is happening behind them.

"So am I getting coffee or not?" I ask while pretending boredom, absently running a hand up the back of my neck and putting my weight into the elbow resting on the top of the couch.

She sighs, lurching forward, "Fine."

I wait until she's gone and dive back to the front door, flinging it open and beckoning the others in.

Rachel and Derrick bring the lidded bucket straight to the sitting room, and I keep a look out for Cindy while Jerry moves behind the sofa with a tranquilizing rifle.

The opening of the bucket lid seems buckshot loud in the tense environment.

"Finally I get to hold the cursed book," grins Rachel.

She picks it up, flipping it open.

"I've been dying to look inside it to see what a demon looks like. She never lets me touch this thing."

Cindy:

Getting louder now. I can see a faint light.
   "Help! Somebody please help me!"
   The lid lifts.

Poppet

"Rachel? Thank God."
"Help me, I'm stuck in this box."

Sasha:

Rachel drops the book.

"Paper cut," she explains, when she looks up to see all of us staring at her in alarm.

Derrick stares at the open pages while Rachel sucks her finger.

"Sasha, have you read this?" he asks.

"Some of it, why?"

"It claims it's Cindy in here," he says.

"What?" Rushing back to the centre of the sitting room, I look at the page.

Help. Rachel! I'm stuck in here.

Sasha! I can see you! Oh thank God. It was so dark and stuffy in here until you opened the lid. I can breathe!

Please help me out.

Help me!

"What the fuck do you think you're doing?"

Spinning around, I stare wide eyed at Cindy in the doorway with two cups of coffee.

"Abraxas I presume?" I reply, my voice wavering.

Her head twitches unnaturally on her neck while a ruthless cackle saws out of the back of her throat.

Both halt abruptly and the silence is unnerving.

"No," she says with proud arrogance.

Smiling myself now, my game face is front and centre, "I've got your number, demon. I know who you are. I've memorized all seventy-two of your names."

Rachel snatches Djinn up again and plunges it into the bucket of water.

Djinn

Cindy drops the cups, shattering them and scattering scalding coffee over the tiles in the hallway, "You're only drowning her. You're too late for your intervention plan." She takes a step into the room. "What? Did you think I didn't know?"

The laugh morphing into a scream scythes through us, activating animal instinct.

I just want to run.

Swiveling my head from Cindy to Rachel, then the bucket, I don't know what to believe. It could be lying to get us to remove it from the salt water, but if it's not lying, we're killing Cindy.

It's lying. Demons always lie.

Cindy:

The room tilts and the box quickly fills up with water. Listening to them, I understand I'm inside the book now. How the fuck did that happen?

Oh God.

Pushing my head to the top, I struggle to get a last deep pull of air before I'm fully submerged in cold water.

I'm too young to die.

Oh Jesus!

Help!

It burns! The salt water burns like acid through me.

I can see La Comtesse de la Nuit pointing her finger at me, yelling, "It's now or never. It's time for you to choose. You won't get another opportunity like this one." She pales severely, making the rouge on her cheeks highlight like clown's make-up, "Or you will burn. **Burn!**"

The planchette shudders, spelling, 'Don't do it,' before shattering the mirror.

Sasha taps the next card, "The Lovers. Harmony and union,

Poppet

choices to be made using intuition and not intellect. Difficult decisions to be made not necessarily about love. Some form of test and consideration about commitments. Abstract thought, internal harmony and union, second sight. Possibly a struggle between two paths."

A struggle between two paths. I didn't realise the paths were demon and human. Fighting for the same body.

My body.

The tarot card of the Moon, "Losing control of one's daily life. The unconscious mind."

The High Priestess, again. This time reversed. **Repression and ignorance of true facts and feelings**. In women, an inability to come to terms with other women or themselves. **Things and circumstances are not what they seem.**

The warnings were all there. Why does hindsight and insight always happen when it's too late?

I see myself floating above the bed, Sasha gripping my ankles, and I'm screaming, "Burn it!"

Why the hell didn't he listen?

Heather hovering in Sasha's lounge, her eyes rolled back, growling, "You're all going to die."

Swallowing water, my lungs are burning.

The Comtesse points at me, "Burn!"

Sasha:

Jerry pops up behind the couch, aiming the dart barrel at her, pulling the trigger. Hurled into the air, I brain myself on the light before knocking the wind out of myself slamming into the floor.

Plan B.

Rolling over, Rachel's got her head in the bucket, convulsing like she's running out of air and drowning, Derrick's comatose and doing a hot air balloon impression, Jerry has the dart sticking out of his neck, slumped over the chair he was behind.

"Looks like it's just the two of us, cowboy," she says.

Turning back, she's standing over me.

Fuck. Here we go again.

"Do you hear those prayers? They piss me off. They alerted me to your plan. I knew you were coming," she sneers.

THUD THUD.

"Open up! This is the police!"

"How are you going to explain luring law enforcement into a death trap? I'm framing you Sasha. You'll look so hot in orange."

I'm ready for this, I have the right name to bind this prick's ass forever. "Memsa-"

Swinging upright, I'm fast forwarded into the doorframe. Pain explodes straight down my spine, desperate to get breath, blood from my nose and mouth asphyxiate me.

I'm pounded over and over face first into the metal frame, my vision blurs along with the smears of blood and I'm desperate for air.

"I'm a lot older than you boy. If anyone dies today, it's going to be you. Where are my dice? Don't make me kill the shaman too," says Cindy.

THUMP.

SMASH.

"Stay where you are ma'am."

"Put your hands where we can see them!" the other guy yells.

"You are under arrest and have the right to remaaaaain ..."

While I'm helplessly staring, the two officers just drop like autumn leaves from a dying tree, landing in an undignified slump behind her.

She turns calmly and looks at them, and I make a home run slide for the bucket, sucking air into my lungs, hauling out both Rachel and Djinn. A vice strong thrust forces my neck down. Straining, my arms locked at the elbows fighting the power

Poppet

holding my cranium and pushing my head into the bucket, I splutter through blood and mucous, "Memsamechvau I bind you with the power of Haagmahim. I bind you back in this book!"

Bracing myself, the plastic on the bucket's about to give, it flexes unsteadily.

The screaming increases to a banshee screech, but the pressure on my head abates long enough for me to flip sideways, away from the threat of the bucket.

Oh fucking fuck.

She looks like she's hemorrhaging from the inside out. Blood's spewing out of her nose, so fast it's turning her into a bloody mess. It's like the opening of a blood oil well.

The first cop sits up, draws his weapon and struggles to his feet.

Cindy dive bombs like a falling sheet of steel, perfectly flat and backwards, smacking her head on the white tiles, her head bouncing with a dull thud that deadens my hope.

Crawling back to Rachel, I open Djinn. "Cindy?"

It stays blank.

Running on adrenaline fumes, I snatch the book up and haul ass to Cindy.

"Cindy?" I pry an eyelid open while the cop, who doesn't give a shit, handcuffs her while she's unconscious. The iris in her eye is blue.

Operating on divine inspiration, I turn her onto her side, clear water pours out of her mouth like a victim of drowning.

Shoving two fingers into her mouth, I check she hasn't swallowed her tongue, then put the fingers on her neck, feeling for a pulse.

Nothing.

"She's got no heartbeat!" Wildly looking between the two men in uniform, I'm desperate, "Do either of you know CPR?"

The tall guy on the left nods, unearthing latex gloves and a

Djinn

device from pockets like a magician opening his act. He pulls on the gloves and kneels next to me, pushing a red rubber tube into her mouth with a thick plastic lip to place his own mouth on.

"New regulation," he says as if explaining, then he begins the arduous task of resurrecting the woman I may as well have murdered with my own bare hands.

This is all my fault.

I put a loaded book in her hands and it pulled the trigger.

Officer Banks touches my shoulder, "Please step away and give him room to work."

Nodding, I remain frozen two shunts over, watching him pump out water from her lungs with every push on her chest, then exhaling into her mouth, repeating over and over.

I vaguely hear the other officer call for medical assistance. With latent urgency I dive for Rachel, checking her for breathing. She is, thank God.

Then I look up at Derrick, still on the ceiling. With a grim determination I force numb legs to move, striding to retrieve that fucking book. Gripping it, I walk back to the bucket, plunging it in and holding it under, waiting for it to drown the way it drowned Cindy.

Confirmation I'm winning is given when Derrick base dives to the floor, his eyes snap open and a harsh oof of impact forces its way past alert vocal chords.

I offer him a nod when pain filled eyes meet mine, and return to my dead girlfriend.

Officer – I look at his name tag – Schwartz, sits back, extracting the device from her mouth, giving me a 'sorry but I tried' expression.

I roll her onto her side again.

"Come on Cindy. Fight!"

She's too pale. Cherry blood, fresh and glistening, still coats all over her neck and chin. The tears well up in me, my nose

Poppet

overheats and drips, "Please Cindy."

Sitting back, pulling her head onto my lap, I stare up sightlessly at the ceiling, "Please!"

Djinn

Chapter 31

Sasha:

With my sanity shriveling, my shoulders shaking with uncontrollable grief, I beg God, and all the others to help me.
 Cough.
 The blood streaked blond spasms in my lap.
 "She's alive!"
  Wailing sirens become so loud they're carving my brain into pages. Dazed, I'm separated from a violently hacking and spluttering Cindy. Watching her convulse like she's having a fit, it sounds like she's choking. I want to get to her and help her but medics swarm like piranha around us, impersonally carrying my friends away as if they're no more than zombies for a pyre, and I lose sight of her in the chaos. An illogical panic grips me when a swab runs over my face and I'm escorted through buzzing mayhem to an ambulance.
 "Where's Cindy?"
 "Sir, you have severe contusions, please relax back."
 "No! Where's Cindy?!"
 I'm strapped down.
 Fuck!
 Struggling against the containment, desperation overrides reason and purpose. I have to get out of here. "I need to see her!"
 The grim faced dyke puts a needle into a tube hanging above

Poppet

my head like an execution noose, and the world smudges into bright white light and rainbows.

When I open my eyes to investigate the strange noises, they focus on Heather Black and who I assume is her attorney.

"How are you feeling?" she asks softly, leaning forward in her chair to rub my arm.

Um?

Dull.

"Okay," I manage to say through parched lips.

My tongue feels thick.

"You're going to be fine. You just have a lot of swelling, but it will go down, so it looks worse than it is. No bones are broken, or anything serious like that."

"And the others?" I ask.

"Jerry's fine, he was simply tranquilized with his own dart. Derrick has a mild concussion but will be fine, and Rachel is also fine, just a bit shaken up. They're in the waiting room."

"Cindy?" I'm almost too afraid to ask.

"She swallowed a lot of water, they've drained the excess fluid, and she's going be right as flowers again. Both of you are being released today."

"And the cops?" I ask with dread.

"They're both fine. Obviously in shock, but considering the unusual circumstances aren't pressing charges. Cindy will, however, have to undergo psychological evaluation before she's allowed back into society."

"But that wasn't even her."

"We know that, but despite the weird sequence of events, with captured evidence, they need to follow procedure," she says.

The suit behind Heather smiles at me, "The good news is we have the camera footage and the eye witness testimony of two law

Djinn

enforcement officers now on our side of evidence."

"Did it work?" I ask, looking Heather directly in her green eyes.

"Yes."

"How do you know?" I ask.

"We've watched the footage over and over, it definitely worked. Djinn is back in his book, dead hopefully, and Cindy is back in control of her own body." she says.

"Why doesn't she remember?"

"It's like going into a walking coma. We think it's the same person, simply because it's the body of the person we know. But when the demon takes over and drives the body, it was like she was unconscious through those times and completely unaware of what he was doing while in control of her body," she explains.

"Then he must have been in control for weeks, because she doesn't even remember winning the lottery."

"Do you recall her ever having memory blanks, right at the beginning?" she asks.

"Uhm. I'm not sure. I did, though."

She nods, her face set in a distasteful expression, "That comes from sleeping with her. You're lucky he didn't transfer across to you. But you saw it in her eyes, didn't you? The person in her eyes was not her. Right?"

"Yeah. I just thought it was her insane look. No normal person would consider they're interacting with their lover sharing a body with a demon when they lay into you, or themselves. Possession is a myth. It's a tale to drive fear into people by an archaic religion. But you're right, I should have known it wasn't her. Her eyes changed so dramatically along with uncharacteristic psychotic behaviour, I should have had her committed."

"It's a possible explanation for multiple personality disorder. The Bible speaks of Mob, in the book of Luke, he was a man possessed. The disciples were warned about exorcisms, to do them properly, or when the demon returned he'd bring a lot more with him into that body. Yet people scoff at spiritual counsel. Djinn is a mental illness, it's a spiritual illness, and both parts of the person have to be healed. Drugs can't give a soul relief from possession," says Heather.

Worming myself up the pillows to look at them, I ask the one thing that makes no sense to me. "Why sea water?"

"If the ocean is powerful enough to bind and hold Leviathan, it's powerful enough to hold Abraxis."

"Cunning bastard having so many names. Even the spelling of Abraxas is thrice different," I grumble.

"Demons have no body, so they have no power here until they get someone to consent to let them use their physical body. But they'd never phrase it so plainly. A book has to be the most unique approach we've witnessed. The Vatican wants a report." Her smile is flat and I feel apprehension mounting again.

"Where's the book now?" I ask.

"Derrick and Rachel took a drive on highway 101, and threw it into the ocean at Devil's Cauldron."

"Good. The cliffs there mean no one will be finding it accidentally," I nod.

She rubs my arm again, "We'll leave you to get dressed. We're happy to drive you home."

"It's okay, I think I'll go with Jerry, but thanks."

As soon as they leave, I dive unsteadily out of the bed and yank on my clothes. I want to see her.

I find her sitting on a chair outside a doctor's room, after going from nurses station to station like a detective to locate her.

She's staring intently at the floor, the world around her shut out. Sitting on the chair next to hers, I slip her hand into mine. "Hey."

Djinn

Sad eyes watch me and her chin begins a wobble, "Are you okay? You look like you lost a fight with Bruce Lee."

"I'm gonna be fine. How are you?"

"I don't know. Physically I'm fine, but inside ..." She looks down, hiding her face from me.

"What?" I pry, squeezing her hand with encouragement.

"Inside I feel like I've lost something precious. It's all bleak and twilighty in here." She thumps her chest with tightly clenched knuckles, sounding as empty as she says she feels.

I wait for her to look up. Eventually she does. "I'm sorry, Cindy. I'm sorry I ever gave you Djinn."

Shit.

I stare in dismay at the sudden mass of tears that spring up unbidden.

"I saw the evidence. I'm so sorry for all the horrific things I did to you," she mumbles.

"It wasn't you."

"I remember only one incident when I could see through my eyes, but had no control. There was no dialogue with him. I was screaming at him to stop." A scary sob belches out of her. "I saw the heartache in your eyes." Looking down again she retracts her hand and balls both fists over her eyes, "I destroyed us."

Watching her, I have a boulder of a lump in my throat.

"We're going to get through this," I whisper, wrapping an arm around her shoulders and pulling her in for a hug. "I know more now. It wasn't you. We're both to blame."

She tries to pull away but I won't let her. I only release her when the doctor calls her in for her psyche results.

Dutifully waiting outside the glass door, I wish I could see a window. This place feels like a prison.

Poppet

Sasha:

I'm immediately awake when she sits up, quaking the bed and gasping.

"What is it?"

"Nightmare," she says.

In my home there is a lamp on both bedside tables. Switching mine on, I roll to stare at her, reaching out to caress her angular shoulder, "Want to share?"

She nibbles her lip, staring at me with accusatory eyes, "Did you date a blond woman?"

"You're blond."

"I dreamed I saw you with a cute blond woman in a cream suit, sitting having coffee in your old kitchen. Your smile was so happy," she says.

"How is that a nightmare?"

"It feeds my insecurities. I got the impression we were over and you were moving on."

"How often did you follow me?" I ask.

"What are you talking about?"

"You deleted all the messages off my phone from Rachel and Heather."

"I did?" She tents her legs, wrapping arms around them and giving me a doubtful look.

"It sounds like you saw me the day I bought this place," I explain.

"Who's the blond?"

"Sybil Smith, my realtor."

"And you didn't ..?" she mumbles.

"Are you naturally this insecure?"

"Answer me."

"Cindy, no, I didn't. Don't stereotype me," I say.

"To answer the insecurity question, no. I never gave a shit

Djinn

either way. I was happy to be single." She scowls at the hemp curtains, "I don't know what the hell is wrong with me." She glances my way, "Or why I'd be so afraid I'd lose you."

"You did lose me, maybe that's what your subconscious fears will happen again."

She squirms over, cuddling up against me. "How long before I don't give a damn?"

"You're never going to be the exact same person you were. If anything, I think this episode has made you more sensitive." I tuck her closer, "Which is a good thing."

"Maybe I need to take up yoga, so I can learn to relax."

"How about we go for some acupressure and acupuncture tomorrow? Have you ever tried it?" I ask.

"No, never."

"Let's do it."

"Okay," she smiles up at me.

It's heart warming having her back; the old Cindy, the one with a gentle pixie smile and mischievous eyes.

"And I promise I'll never use an oracle again. No Ouija boards, pendulums, spiritualist churches, books, cards, runes, none of it," she says. "I even trashed my magic box."

"Yeah, I concur. I'm good to just live in Happy Valley and be content living day to day." But now I'm curious, "You had a magic box?"

"It was silly and stupid. I'm no longer interested in dabbling with the occult," she says.

"Good. We have Heather to thank for helping us through that, even though a normal person would have been isolated with their grief, she was a real soldier."

"I guess. She's a God reccie. Engaged in a private war no one else knows about."

I relish her warmth, speaking my mind, "It's good to have you back."

Poppet

"After all the things I allegedly did, I'm surprised I'm not a wanted woman."

Nibbling her neck, I refuse to let the opportunity slide, "You are a wanted woman."

Cindy:

I have a thousand needles sticking out of me, precariously, when my cell phone rings.

"Can I answer that?" I ask the lady with the magic hands.

"Yes, just don't move," she says, handing me the phone.

"Hello?" I say after accepting the call, putting it on speaker and talking through the face hole in the table.

"Cinders! How are you doing girl?" says Rachel.

"I'm good, I even think I could possibly be happy. You?"

"I dunno. Derrick and myself are fine, but I can't stop thinking about that book," she says.

"What about it?"

"It seems like such a shame to throw something that rare into the ocean. Shouldn't it be in a museum or something?"

"No. It should be lost to mankind forever," I say.

"Oh –" she falters.

"Why?" I ask suspiciously.

"No reason. So what are you up to?"

"Acupuncture, right this second."

"We should catch up soon. I won't keep you. I have another call to make anyway," she says.

"Oh yeah, who is he?"

She laughs, and it's her nervous laugh. "I'm thinking of taking up mountaineering. It's time to learn survival skills, like how to scale sheer rock."

"Why the hell would you need that?"

"You do your weird stuff, it's my turn," she counters.

Djinn

"Just don't fall and break your neck."

She laughs again, "Stay cool girlfriend."

"You too."

"Bye."

I hang up and ponder the strange call from Miss Anti-Djinn. That was outright weird.

Leaving the An Sen clinic, which means 'peaceful heart', we take the elevator down and walk to the car in a day so perfect it should be a 'wish you were here' postcard.

He directs the hybrid Honda from SE Washington Street, directly eagle direction, we then turn into SE Martin Luther King Jnr Boulevard, bringing back strong memories for both of us.

A little later we're happily relaxing at Loyla on SE 21st Avenue. Meeting Sasha in the steam room wearing nothing but our fluffy cotton gowns, I watch him through the haze.

"Just spill it. Something is eating you."

"How do you know me so well?" I can't help grinning.

"I haven't a clue."

I love his hair shorter and spiky. It's more mature and suits him.

"Well?" he pushes.

"Rachel phoned me just now."

"Yeah?"

"Mmm, and she said the weirdest thing."

"What?"

"She asked me about Djinn. She thinks it's a shame it's in the ocean and thinks it should be in a museum or something. But I thought she hated that book?"

"That is odd. Does Derrick know?" he says.

"Probably." I chuckle, telling him, "And now she's taking up

Poppet

mountaineering."

"Wow, way left field."

Except he's shoving his fingers through his hair, the way he does when he's worrying.

"Sasha, what? What did I say?"

"I just remembered something."

"About me?"

What else could I have done? I hate that demon. I'll hate him forever.

"No, about her. When she opened Djinn, she got a paper cut."

We stare at each other with instant apprehension, "Blood bond," we say in unison.

"Shit," he says, grabbing my hand and hauling us out of the steamroom.

As we enter the central room, he says, "I have to go and testify for Heather later today anyway. We'll get her to go with us. I'm not hesitating on this intervention."

I stop him, yanking his arm and making him stop rushing. He looks impatiently at me, and I wind both arms around his waist, staring up, "Thank you for being my hero."

"I dunno Cin–"

I interrupt him, "Remember the card you drew on our first date? You are my King of Wands. You said; King of Wands. A charming, responsible, loyal, entertaining, witty, honest, conscientious and generous person. A lover of the home and family life. A very passionate and virile man who is good at moral support and encouragement. When pushed or provoked he acts without hesitation, but can sometimes find this hard as he can often see both sides of an argument."

"Cindy, now's not the time ..."

"Now is the perfect time. I love you, for being you. Heaven sent you to me, and they almost converted me they did such a good job."

Djinn

His grin is boyish and self-conscious.

"You're going to give me a big head."

I laugh suggestively, letting that hang between us before we commit to rescuing Rachel from Abraxas.

Sasha:

She loved the Scandinavian vibe of Loyly, and wouldn't leave until she had a bag of natural and organic Dr Hauschka skin-care products. I think I've completely converted her into a tree hugger.

Absently running a palm up her leg, I give her a grin. We're alive, we made it. It takes twenty minutes of Indian drumming companionship through the speakers before I take the exit for Sunnybrook Boulevard. I love this album, it reminds me of how much we owe Jon Spotted Eagle for his insight and wisdom. Without him I would never have known she had the dice and she'd still have a link to Abraxas.

Glancing at her, I ask, "So what shop should I open next?"

"None. I need you more than anyone else does."

"You're going to get bored of me really soon," I say, driving through our old haunts on SE Powell boulevard, past McDonald's and Goodwill's, beyond Burgerville, Wing's food market, and Shell, before turning right into SE 129th Avenue.

"Let's go to Tibet, Machu Picchu, the pyramids, let's just go adventuring, who cares about having a job? We could spend our lives having fun."

Turning right as we drive past stands of fir trees into SE Mountain Gate road, we drive uphill on the picturesque road, past rock retaining walls, and directly left into Evening Star and my home base.

I tease her, "Just don't you dare come home with any artifacts. Leave them the hell alone."

Poppet

She laughs indulgently, "Have no fear."

Stopping in the driveway with a sense of overwhelmed homecoming, I take my phone out of the handset. "We'll change, then go to the courthouse for Heather, then from there we can all go to Rachel and Derrick's place?"

She nods, gifting me with her combustible smile, "Yes captain."

Getting out of the vehicle, I dial Derrick. Sifting through my keys, she beats me to it, opening the front door with her own set of keys.

We share a 'couple madly in love' smile when Derrick answers.

"Yo, Derrick. Sash here. We need to talk."

~☆ **The End** ☆~

Djinn

Poppet

Djinn

I'd like to thank Jeff Blackmer for being my Portland guru and beta reader.

Thank you also to Simon Corbin and Terry Golding for being beta readers and proof readers, your opinions have been invaluable to me.

Thank you also to the rock band Surrounded By Idiots, from New Jersey USA, for allowing me the use of their song.

And thank you to Chic for spotting mistakes no one else did.

Poppet

The greatest gift you can give any author, is a book review.

Please consider leaving a book review on any popular book website where your favorite author is sold.

From all authors, and myself, thank you.

Djinn

Made in the USA
San Bernardino, CA
04 March 2013